Albyn Leah Hall was born in  lived in London since 1984.

Other 90s titles

Keverne Barrett   *Unsuitable Arrangements*

Neil Bartlett   *Ready to Catch Him Should He Fall*

Suzannah Dunn   *Darker Days Than Usual*

James Lansbury   *Korzeniowski*

Eroica Mildmay   *Lucker and Tiffany Peel Out*

Silvia Sanza   *Alex Wants to Call it Love*

Susan Schmidt   *Winging It*

Mary Scott   *Not in Newbury* and *Nudists May Be Encountered*

Atima Srivastava   *Transmission*

Lynne Tillman   *Absence Makes the Heart*

Colm Tóibín   *The South*
  (Winner of the 1991 *Irish Times* Aer Lingus Fiction Prize)

Margaret Wilkinson   *Ocean Avenue*

deliria

albyn leah hall

This volume was published with assistance from the
Ralph Lewis Award at the University of Sussex

Library of Congress Catalog Card Number: 93–83066

A CIP catalogue record for this book is available
from the British Library on request

First published 1993 by
Serpent's Tail, 4 Blackstock Mews, London N4
and 401 West Broadway #1, New York, NY 10012.

Set in 10½/14pt Goudy by Contour Typesetters, Southall, London
Printed in Great Britain by Cox & Wyman Ltd,
Reading, Berkshire

Dedicated to . . .

Abigail Thomas
Thomas Godfrey
Lynn Pleshette

Grateful acknowledgement is made to the following for use of song lyrics:

Barney Rush/ Mild Music for 'Nancy Spain'
MacGowan Music/Perfect Songs for
   'A Pair of Brown Eyes' and 'Lullaby of London'
Christy Moore/BAL Music and Mattie Fox Management for
   'Delirium Tremens' and 'The Knock Song'

decor

When asked what frightens me most about London, I say, it is not the pinwheeled eyes of junkies on the street. Their craggy faces are as safe as old bark to me; they are but remnants of a petrified forest I have left behind.

It is not the looming tyranny of prefab structures, square and scowling down on treeless roads of cracked cement, strangled shrubberies and dull-hued minis all in a row. London frowns in its own colours. I dignify it with titles stolen from tidy strips of paint samples, one ambling shopping-Sunday: Rembrandt brown for the autumn and brownstone brown, nighthawk brown, toasted spice, redcurrant, jasper, romany, marmalade. Hastings green or Essex pink for the summer. Gypsy rose and jamboree for the spring. Lord Richard grey, flint grey, arctic shadow and smokestone grey the whole year round. It makes me feel better to do this. Less afraid. Not that I am afraid of sprigs and shades; I like the detail, the city smells. I would never cry at the sight of a battered Rover, nor shiver in the sad vacancy of a council estate. I say to my friends, see the romance in it, the history. See it juxtaposed: the Heath in winter and the slums in May. And if they say 'Go fuck yourself,' then they are probably right, for I am lying. But in a way, I'm not.

What frightens you most about London? Asks a kind of friend who knows me well. Is it the sullen sky, small and mean in winter, the rank dank smell of piss sharp through your nostrils when you walk below the tracks at Gospel Oak or beneath the highway in the Edgware Road?

No, I say. Not at all. It is my hot little bedroom, heavy with mildew and mauve, and most of all, it is the bed. It is the lint and fluff on my old winter coat, stuck to the sleeves like dead bugs, and it is the same old towel hanging from the rack in my bathroom, stiff with decay but still pink, still the shape it was over a year ago, the last time I used it, the last time I shoved it across my stubborn wet flesh and up between my legs and rough through my tangle of sopping hair, the same hair, the same hair. It is the smell of Pears shampoo and Mum deodorant leaking milky white through the armpits of my blouse. It is the heavy brass diamonds upon my window, the security grilles; when did I put them there? *Did I* put them there? I lie in my bed and stare at the cracked plaster in the ceiling, the smudges of handprints (how in the hell did they get there?), and I wonder why I am so afraid. Sure, the bathroom door is weak with misalignment and it will not shut. Sure, there are no working clocks in the entire flat, just one lively broken green thing that ticks happily as if it could tell the time, though the second hand only pulses and stays in one place. Sure, the sheets are coarse and dusty like the head of a kitchen matchstick. But these are only things. I think to myself, if the walls were ivory instead of mauve, and if I put fine ash floorboards down where the fat grey carpet used to be, would I then be happy and unafraid? I might. I make plans and lists. I purchase *Elle Decoration* and French *Casa Vogue* from my local newsagent. I phone carpenters and painters, and a funny little man with glasses to dig up my garden. I light a stick of sage and run through the flat with it, as I am told that it will dismember the evil spirits, like an exterminator murders termites and then removes them. I do not know if the gesture is valid, but I enjoy the ritual; it makes me feel better. The guys from 'Love that Wall' decorators arrive. They stand around with rulers and clipboards. They say, 'You have serious subsidence in your study.' They say, 'Don't know about those neon lights, they're sort of an acquired taste. At the end of the day, you want something sunny and cheerful, something that'll make you smile when you walk in the room.' 'When can you start?' I ask. They tell me they will send an estimate. It may take a week or two. They're busy. 'It's a busy time. Choose your colours carefully. At the end of the day, you want to be sure.'

So I lie in my bed in that same old bedroom, for there is nowhere else, just now, to lie. And I stare at the handprints on the ceiling. The bathroom door swings open and the light is on, the bare bright bulb. The stiff pink towel glares at me, contorted and frozen like a hunchback caught in the ice. I do not turn off the bathroom light. I do not shut the bathroom door. I stare at the towel and I am frightened.

strange fruit

It is a sick-making autumn. Crilly and I spend all our time in bed.
Our lovemaking is long and moist, dozy and grave, but
afternoons leave me frazzled and dizzy. Even the inside of a
plastic bag makes me want to vomit, with its musty smell of
lumber or the back room of a small shop. I spend much of my
time at the shops; wandering through the aisles, faltering, never
knowing what to buy. I knock things off the shelves. The old
Pakistani gentleman, his face lined and patient, puts a basket in
my hand and says, you need this, you drop things. I don't cook
much. We have meals of tuna fish, instant noodle soup, baked
beans. And chocolate. Late night Mars or Marathon bars from
the petrol station. Heavy foods are soothing with their easy,
empty calories; we are lovers full of sugar, we are higher than the
ceiling.

I do not worry about the vomiting — it comes naturally. That
is, it seems natural. It erupts, rattles, and disposes of itself. It's
nice to vomit. It leaves my skin flushed, my eyes bright, revelling
in the cool relief afterwards. It is a gentle cycle, and circular
things give justice and symmetry; they make me calm. Crilly is
concerned at the state of me. He tries to comfort me. There is
no need. I tell him so. We keep each other awake all night with
our bodies, our food, our sex and, of course, the other. The days
are more difficult.

My periods come and go. I have never been regular, so it is not
disturbing to find them light, blotchy and short-lived.

Menstrual blood leaves me, but the sickness persists. I am doing an art course, but I never go. There are calls from college. There is bed. Crilly thieves and cons to procure the evening's comfort. I have no energy. My friends ask questions. I elude them; my friends, that is, and the questions they ask.

I fly away at Christmas. I go to California, and my family. I am away for four weeks. The first week is hell; jet lag and a sluggish nausea I can't explain. I am visited by dense and dreamless sleep before the horrific wakefulness; hours in which I do nothing but watch.

. . . Evangelists in Florida, wasp-green eyes reckless, un-blinking, black spiders haunt the pink lids of preachers' wives, upholstered in satin stripes. Commercials for cellulite products on early morning cable, cheaply lit and noisy, feel your thighs and buy our cream, thousands of buyers interviewed, send away. Do it now. Everything frightens me. It is not death I fear, but dying, and the hallucinations I will have in its wake. Shivering through to my wrists and nipples, I know it is not jet lag.

Eventually, I recover, and come to enjoy my mother and my old school friends, and the easy, sunny inertia of L.A. I swim every day and I love the blue sparkle of the pool, the glare of the sun and the sky on the water, and myself cleansed and pristine in the chlorinated wet of my morning routine, pre-smog, post-dope; boys with blond moustaches saying, 'Have a good one'; my baby blue Rent-a-car. I take to the freeways. I am alive at last. I resolve to leave my stagnant Irish lover. I will be crippled no longer, I tell my friends. I am precious about my newfound solitude. I'll leave him promptly upon my return to England. He meets me at Heathrow. I leave him that night.

A week later, I am making amends at college, working out at the gym, and seeing people-friends who do not, to my astonishment, resent me. They say I have only flirted with a temporary vice and its vice-keeper and, having survived them both, I am still me and I am no junkie. I visit their homes. They visit mine. I frequent pubs and clubs and brasseries, the neglected poky holes of single social living; watching the fat flamenco dancer weave her way across tables at the Spanish bar, eating tapas at four in the morning. It is February. I am twenty-four. I even enjoy the shrill nagging pierce of my alarm, and slumber no longer claims me like the flu.

Sometimes I wake early to beat the clock. I speak of Crilly and the fool that he is. A poor, tragic creature. Weak. Besotted. Missing me. I picture him in the back of his friend's flat where he is staying. I see him sluggish and stoned in my mind's eye, his ginger hair and heavy lidded eyes, his clammy, groping hands and nothing to call his own. I hate him. I come home later to hear his voice on my answerphone; slow and heavy, pleading, knackered. His accent as broad as it ever was. Forever a desolate Dublin man.

I do not sleep with other men. Only once do I allow a man to stay the night, and I make him sleep upstairs. We stay up most of the night, discussing music. He is that disdainful sort of 'artist' who is gaunt and fine-featured and born to be better. He is a dedicated musician. He teaches me one of his songs and I sing it while he plays the guitar. He knows Crilly, slightly; he says that for guys like Crilly, he shows no mercy. He will not stop talking, drinking cups of coffee. I make them, despite a stirring strangeness in my stomach. There are so many places he's been, so many gigs he's done. He has tried heroin, but risen swiftly above it. I begin to despise him. At two o'clock, the phone rings.

Crilly calls me 'Jezebel', and sometimes he calls me 'Jez'. His voice is low.

He asks me how I am. Great, I tell him. He apologises for phoning so late. He tells me that I sound strange, just a little strange, as strange as the time of night. I say I am fine and hang up. There is little I can say. I fetch a duvet for my guest, and I go to bed alone.

A few days later, I look at myself in the mirror. My stomach is strange, as though something has tilted inside it. Something more obtrusive than last night's supper. I stop at the Health Centre on my way to the gym. There is no doctor free to see me, but a nurse takes a sample of urine. She is kind. She speaks with an Irish accent; a country accent, not like Crilly's. I wait five and then ten minutes in a cubicle. I sit high on a table with a white paper sheet on it. I swing my legs. I think of when I was very small and lived in New York. My mother took me to a paediatrician on the East Side of town, once or twice a year. He had a waiting-room full of strange, swinging objects; animals with rounded bottoms rocking on a clean, shiny floor, while children played and young mothers looked on.

The nurse returns and sits facing me. 'I think we have a baby,' she says, and feels my stomach. 'Four or five months by the look of it. How could you not have known?'

'There was some bleeding,' I tell her. 'I had periods,' though upon reflection, the bleeding does seem mean and scarce, and I cannot exactly remember my last period. I have blamed the sickness on smack and there is something simple and hygienic about this; my womb has nothing to do with it. The nurse is elderly and lovely; a matron out of dreams. She touches my arm.

'It does happen, sometimes,' she says. 'Blood can come at any time.'

I phone Crilly in the afternoon. I ask him to meet me that evening at the Three Pigeons. I go to the gym in spite of myself, puffing and plodding along. The treadmill is the hardest, but I keep on. I feel a lively lump inside of me and a need to keep it vital; to keep on running though I am panting and sweating like a sore animal; to encase it in life, to keep it moving. Deadish flesh hangs from all parts. I run to remove it. The sweat is good — like shedding poison. I run in repentance.

No.

I feel a dead lump inside me, a parcel of old and tired meat; I run to destroy it, to spare it the misery of what will come, I run out of mercy, to quicken its demise. I imagine its removal, my womb collapsing to follow, closing it on itself like a ball of orange peels without the fruit.

I doll myself up at dusk. I paint my face, cover myself in beads. I wear rosary beads from Mexico, bought from a veiled old lady in a church.

When I arrive at the Three Pigeons, Crilly twirls me about to look at me. He buys me a double Jameson's. We sit together in the wooden booth. I keep my distance and do not look at him, though from the corner of my eye I can see him so smartly attired, decked out in scarves and jumpers, set to brace the cold and the street at any hour. I am about to tell him when Henry arrives, sickly and sniffling.

'Have you seen Perry?' he asks. 'Maggie said you were in here. I thought Perry might be with you.'

'No.' Crilly is contemptuous of Henry, but the latter sits beside us just the same, not buying a drink but sniffing and staring dully out of eyes deadish and glazed. Suddenly, he starts.

'Oy!' he says, 'Do you want to buy some jumpers?' He reaches for a plastic bag. 'Lovely lambswool, from the Shetlands. Rare. Got loads of them. What do you think?' Henry holds the jumpers up for us to see.

We shake our heads. Henry sits back and closes his eyes. Ten minutes later, he asks us again. His hair is greasy and his face is wet with perspiration. 'They're prime choice these things. Do you want them? I'll give you a fine price seeing it's you and yours. They are rare and pure . . .'

Perry strides into the pub, formidable as ever, following his long Roman nose, his hair black with rain and his blue eyes ablaze from the cold, among other things. He wears a long trenchcoat. Henry jumps up and tries to steer him away. He wants Perry all to himself. Well, we all do. 'Perry you handsome paddy!' he cries. 'Where the fuck have you been?'

Perry extricates himself and takes a chair across from us. 'It's grand to see the two of youse together,' he says, cool as you like. Then softly, leaning into us: 'Will I be serving youse?'

I turn to face Crilly for the first real time. He is holding his breath. He looks at Perry, then at me. I give nothing away.

'We'll be with you in a minute,' he says. 'Take care of that pratt while you're at it. He's desperate.' Henry stands in the corner, too expectant to be rude. He seems to be panting. Perry reluctantly recedes until we can no longer hear either of them, though we watch Henry gesticulate, wiping sweat from his mouth and brow, pausing only to sniffle. Perry only nods. Crilly gives a short laugh. 'He's a dozy cunt, that Henry,' he says. From time to time, Perry glances at us. I admire him; so striking. Always the man you're looking for. Mmm. Crilly is not blind to my admiration.

'Shall I leave?' he says.

I laugh. 'Don't be stupid,' I snap, and I suck on my Jameson's.

'Are you ever going to tell me what's wrong?'

I think about it for a moment. I look at him and take his hand. I put it on my stomach. Crilly's eyes grow wide. He takes me in his arms and holds me. I do not feel anything much. Perry is rid of his pursuer, fresh again. He stands near the door, waiting for us.

'What will we do, Jez?'

I look at Crilly.

'What will we do?'

Crilly is stern and sad. I look back at the door.

I say we'll do what we always do. Crilly does not stir. He gazes hard into my face, as though hoping I will change my mind. The bell rings, closing time. After another moment or two, Crilly takes my arm and leads me from the pub. We leave with Perry, in my car.

We wait in different places; the car park of an estate, a street corner in Archway. Crilly and I sit in my living-room with a roll of silver foil before us, listening to Van Morrison; the cat an audible purring ball on my lap. Crilly fixes us up with a brown powdered lump upon the foil. He hands me the silver tube, lights a match and holds it under the foil while I suck in and follow the smoke. It has been six weeks, almost, but the friendly hot flush fills me to the top of my head and it is beautiful. Crilly makes popcorn for us. I roll a joint and turn off the bright neon, leaving us with the sultry lilac glow of a smaller and older lamp, the first I ever bought. We think of it as 'aqua-velvet'. Crilly says that it turns the place into a nightclub, in the Caribbean. From the outside, a passerby will gaze up at the window, and all he will see is that lavender light.

He kisses me now, cautiously, as I might refuse. He eases me to the floor. 'Jasus how I've missed you,' he says. He tastes of salt. He puts his hands on my stomach. 'Is he there?'

I move his hand until it feels correct. 'There,' I say. 'I can feel it when I sit.'

Crilly touches me all over with one hand, keeping the other on my stomach. He holds my breasts. 'Who do they belong to?' he asks, and I throw my head back, enjoying the rhetoric. He reaches between my legs. 'Who does that belong to?' he asks, and I squeeze my legs together as though to resist him, and it feels good; so good that my back arches. He again holds my lower stomach. 'Who does that belong to?'

I allow him to explore. 'He's yours,' I say, and he pins my wrists to the floor. Crilly has a bracelet which makes a noise like keys. It rattles about my ears and head. I feel dizzy. I rub myself up against him. 'He's yours as long as he's here.' I'm whispering now. 'Don't get any ideas about having me back again.'

I do not think I am being cruel. I feel excited and I tingle everywhere. Crilly stops and stares at me, and then stands looking ginger and flushed, and he gathers his things. He does not wait for me to protest but slams the door behind him as he leaves, leaving a £20 bag on the coffee table in his haste.

At the clinic, there is a chip-toothed, pink-faced sliver of a thing with lank highlighted hair and huge rabbit eyes. She calls herself Jackie and she shares my room. She is nineteen weeks pregnant, as I am. Happily, our foetuses are small, and we can expect a standard termination. We are grateful to escape the alternative. The room we share is not large, but we are divided from one another by a plastic curtain.

Anita drives me to Twickenham Clinic at seven. I have seen Crilly once or twice since telling him, but our meetings were brief and stilted. I cannot remember whether he has arranged to visit me at Twickenham. All practical things are settled between Anita and myself. She drives me in my car and we do not say much.

I sit in the waiting-room for over an hour. I watch the women arrive with their carrier bags, their boyfriends, husbands, mothers. Eventually, I am called to the front to pay my fee. A nurse takes me down a corridor into a white room with painted-shut windows and a hot-air vent. I take the bed by the wall, behind the curtain. I hang my clothes in the wardrobe and put on the plastic gown. I walk on tiptoe. The floor is hot and shiny. Affixed to the wall at a considerable height is a small television on a swivel, facing the bed. I turn it on.

At first, Jackie does not appear to notice me. She wears a pink suede jacket with a studded fringe which she takes great care to hang. Her lurex leggings, high suede boots and yellow sweatshirt are folded and tucked away with equal care. She gets into bed.

She reads Harold Robbins. She asks the nurse if her husband has left. She speaks with a broad London accent. She is nasal, but she is not loud.

A second nurse takes my blood pressure and checks my pulse. She gives me a valium. She tells me to rest. I keep the television on. I keep it low.

In the operating theatre, a tall and ancient nurse jabs me twice to find the vein in the back of my hand. She sounds Dutch. 'How am I to do this,' she orders, 'if you keep moving like an animal?' There is a great gush of pain as the needle goes in, deep at last. Veins convulse everywhere in my arm, so shot full of liquid I am sure they will burst. If I shut my eyes, they surely will. I fight to keep them open. The stream is cold and cutting. Despite my struggle, sleep comes at once.

I am awakened by the cramps. Low and rumbling they are, like the threat of an earthquake or hurricane. I am wheeled back to my room. Once in motion, they erupt with abandon. I cry out as if to keep them outside of myself. They persist and grow stronger. I double up in halves, clinging to my knees. The nurse shifts me from the cart to the bed with some difficulty. From a few feet away, I hear a doctor speaking.

'This is the contraction of the womb,' he says, in a shout or a murmur. 'In pregnancies as far along as yours, one's womb will expand and then contract after the termination, causing some pain and discomfort. It is bound to contract.'

I picture in my mind the womb, small and malleable as the heart muscle, expanding and contracting at ludicrous speed. I laugh and then I shriek.

Someone shuts the curtain. 'You don't feel anything, do you?' a nurse asks Jackie, on the other side.

'Fit as a fiddle, darlin,' and I can hear, faintly, through the twisted frenzy of my own pelvis, a cheerful rustle as she turns the pages of her magazine. I am plagued by awkward thoughts, like splinters in my brain: the seventh grade and pocket radios, games of spin the bottle from which I am cheerfully excluded, tight jeans, Bonnie Bell lip gloss, me, boyish and baffled, the menacing breath of puberty. I count to myself. I pretend I am in a crib in a wood with the sky above me. I pretend I am at my father's in the spring of my eighth year, staying awake late together, the two of us, miles past bedtime, eating cold takeout spaghetti from the local Italian deli, watching *My Man Godfrey* on hastily edited late night television, the tiny room dark but for the flicker of a tatty late night screen, our tired eyes bleary but soft, placid, from feeding. I think of a time, not long after I met Crilly, in bed together, bound by tight covers. He read to me from Brendan Behan's *The Borstal Boy*. The pain subsides.

When it has gone completely, I venture up a flight of stairs in my bare feet to the phone box. There is a small queue of groggy creatures in hospital gowns. The girl speaking is small with stringy hair tied back in a knot, and glasses. She wears a nightdress of her own, a faded pattern of lilacs. 'I know it's a long way,' she is saying, 'I've never been here myself, before today. Please try to come, try and make it down.'

When it is my turn to use the phone, I stand for a minute with two ten pence coins in my hand. I cannot remember who to call. I think of several people. I consider a few. Roger in his comfortable jacket, his hair receding and long at the back, the foetal guitar in his arms, singing a song about buffalo. Pamela, in a cloud of artistic dust and her fine finished features; Anita, sensible, eating salad. No. I put the coin in and dial my own number. I don't know why; only that I want to hear my voice on the answerphone. But when I get through, even my own voice sounds strange and mechanical; an air hostess for British Airways, an operator for British Telecom. I hang up and ring Crilly at his friend's flat. I am met by another answerphone with the friend's voice on it. I leave a message for Crilly. I tell him I am fine. I say I am bored, and that I hope to see him that evening. I am only bored. I repeat the address of the clinic several times. I ask him to bring a packet of wholemeal digestives. I speak in a drone.

'I know it's a long way,' I say, 'I don't even know which line to take on the underground. You'll have to look at a map. You'll have to look at a map, a map on the wall in the tube. Or ask someone which line to take. Ask the man in the tube . . .'

The pips come. I am alone on the stairwell. Through a doorway, the glare of a television light reflects upon somebody's wall. As I pass, I see the girl with glasses as she sits in her bed; her spectacled eyes flashing bulbs on the screen.

I return to my bed. I open the curtain separating Jackie and myself. I ask her if she has any special preferences as far as the telly is concerned. She says that she doesn't mind either way, though she wouldn't say no to *Neighbours* at 5.30, as we have missed the 1.30 episode. We discuss the soaps. I have one or two which I watch faithfully, but she likes them all. She explains that though she works most days, there is a television where she works. She owns a video shop with her husband, in Mile End.

She gives me her key-ring to look at; a plastic heart in which a photo of her husband and two children are encased. Her hands drop to her stomach, clutching her absent bulge. 'We're skint,' she says. 'We can't afford another. And you?'

'I'm not sure what happened,' I say after awhile.

We are vague and polite with one another. It seems the best way to be.

By three o'clock, Jackie and I are ravenous. Lunch is a sparse plate of sandwiches with salmon paste or paper-thin processed turkey roll. Jackie goes upstairs to phone her husband at work, so that he might make a trip to the shops before visiting hour. I settle back in my bed to read, but I am startled by a wetness between my legs.

In the bathroom, I remove the sanitary napkin and belt I have been dressed with, while still unconscious, after the operation. Blood gushes forth like nothing I have seen from my own body. It is all over the toilet seat and the floor. It seeps between my toes and the cracks in the floor tiles. I fetch a handful of paper towels from beside the wash basin, walking on tiptoe to avoid bloody footprints. There seems a great distance between the toilet and the wash basin. I get on my knees and manage to wipe away nearly all of the blood, though some of it sticks stubbornly in the crevices of the floor. I dampen more towels and scrub the whole of my legs and feet, though I cannot remove it all, and much of it smears into my skin, giving it a pinkish tint. I think of lipstick samples at Bullocks department store, the way you rub the lipstick from your lips and it stains your hand the whole day through.

When I return to the room, Jackie sits upright in her bed, her books and magazines stacked neatly by her side.

'I've spoken to John,' she tells me. 'He says he will bring us some fruit and biscuits and things. I told him also to get cheese moments and scampi fries, and he may stop at McDonald's.'

'Good,' I say gratefully. 'That's good.'

'Don't mention it,' she says, smiling. 'And knowing John, there'll probably be Jaffa cakes for later.'

And so, hours later, when the room has gone a dusky grey from winter twilight and the smoke of our cigarettes, a most blank and bovine nurse accompanies Jackie's husband into the room, and he indeed bears an armful of Sainsbury's. Both of us having slept and eaten since Jackie's phone call, we are no longer very hungry. I do feel a rumbling deep in my stomach, but it is a restless churning rather than an empty one, much like the overturning of soil by an ambling tractor. It is night. We turn our bedside lamps on. John smiles apologetically at me as he arranges himself at her bedside.

'I thought you were *starving*,' he says to her. He is a tall, stocky chap with a husky voice. He speaks in a tired murmur of business and the kids, dry rot in the house, his brother's pop band. Holding the open gown tightly around myself, I rise to adjust the volume on the television, so that it will not disturb them. 'No, it's all right,' they say, very nearly in unison. They are taking pity. Bitterly, I tug at the curtain, but it remains ajar. Crilly is not coming.

A few minutes later, the very same nurse appears with Crilly behind her, bearing gifts and flowers. He is clean-shaven and well-dressed. The nurse leaves, shutting the door behind her. Crilly comes to my bed and sits beside me. I am stunned to find him so fine and ruddy in the startling, bleak white of this room; so handsome in the face of my decay, my washed-out skin and faded eyes, my smears of blood and perspiration.

'I've brought you your biscuits,' he says, and he puts them in my hand.

'Oh Crilly,' I say. 'I bled and bled. I couldn't stop it!' He holds me close. I pull away and examine his eyes.

'You're dressed for the occasion,' I say sharply. His pupils are large. He is not stoned. I ask, 'Is it a slow night in Camden?' He wants to know what I mean.

'Otherwise,' I say, 'you may not have come.'

Crilly is hurt. My eyes sting. My accusation fills me with shame.

'How could you say such a thing,' he begins, 'With me in bits and pacing the streets like a fockin' animal, with no one but the likes of Perry to pour me heart out to!'

I think of Perry with his mess of black hair and his icy, pinned eyes. Crilly has known Perry since early childhood. Their mums are both nurses at St Ita's Hospital and they play bingo together on Saturdays. According to Crilly, Perry was the last kid in school to wear short trousers. Thinking about it makes me smile.

Crilly relaxes. We laugh a little, at nothing too much. He takes my hand. I tell him about the cramps, feeling like a child who has fallen and cut herself, demanding sympathy. Crilly spares me nothing. He fluffs my pillow and adorns me with trinkets; earrings and a flowery jar of perfume called 'Fire Maiden'.

'I bought it just for a laugh.' He is sheepish. 'The name reminded me of you.' (O yes, me, with my stunned and sallow face, me with my drained and broken lump of a body!)

Crilly strokes my forehead. 'Claudia,' he says, 'I'd be immensely pleased if you'd let me stay with you at your place and take care of you for a while. Just until you're well . . .'

'Or until you are.' I look away.

'I don't mean to be presumptuous,' he continues. 'I'm under no illusions about the two of us, on me mother's life . . .'

His words come in a rush. I suddenly feel very hot. I push his hand from my face. On the other side of the curtain John is saying,

'The little one was wheezing so I kept him home. What did you expect me to do . . .?'

I listen to the sounds of the room. Presently, I return my gaze to Crilly. 'Can you get something special for us?' I ask. 'Just for a few days or so . . . something to ease the pain?'

Crilly smiles like a father. 'Of course,' he says, taking me in his arms. 'Of course,' and I begin to cry then, to really cry, while he whispers in my ear how brave I am, so very brave; the sweet, steady lull of his voice competing only with John and Jackie on the other side of the curtain, while the telly relents upon its silly swivel, hushed though it is, advert upon advert falling on all ears in a quiet, busy murmur.

In the thick of the morning, the cold is shocking. I have half a mind to defy their demands of space and economy, and to sleep on until awakened by the next pale arrival herself, expectant to abort and puzzled at my slumbering presence. I become attached to that firm slab of practical mattress and look upon it as a sort of lily-white oasis cloud in a world of cold and sterile air. I cling to my pillow. A formidable West Indian nurse bellows at me as sure as the rooster himself. She is brazen and loud, correct.

I eat breakfast in a hall full of silent women. A low rumble of a cramp circles deep inside me like a fly, but it remains benign. A slender, tawny-haired girl sits opposite eating cereal, avoiding my eyes. I have seen her before, in a cocktail dress at someone's party, or at an exhibition perhaps. I keep my mouth shut just the same.

After breakfast, I sit in the outgoing waiting-room, facing the door, with Jackie and the women of yesterday morning clutching their knees and their overnight bags, looking pale. One by one, people arrive to fetch them; the mums, the lovers, the friends of before. I recognise them and with each recognition I take some comfort. The door is slow and heavy; we turn our faces up to meet its every clank, entrance, creak, slam. A groggy morning. It is sinfully early.

Crilly isn't long in fetching me. The sound of his bracelet precedes him and he brings a rush of morning chill in. I turn to Jackie. I cannot think of what to say.

'Good luck with your video shop,' I say.

'Thank you.'

Crilly takes my arm and leads me from the clinic, onto the green and into the car where Anita sits at the wheel. He puts me in the back seat with my coat over my knees. Anita asks how I am feeling. I tell her I am tired and giddy from last night's sleeping pill. We drive through Twickenham. Suddenly I am cheerful. Euphoric, even. I lean forward and whisper into Crilly's ear.

'Crilly?' I whisper.

'Yes, angel.'

'You canny shove your granny up a bus!' I sing gaily in a loud Scottish accent. (My friend Simone has taught me this.)

'That's very good, baby,' says Crilly. Anita groans.

'Do you know anyone who lives in Twickenham?' I ask Crilly and Anita, who sit erect in the front seat, like adults. They don't. It is a grey shallow-skied morning. I tell Anita to follow all the signs north.

'I know,' she says, and I know that she knows.

Once in Kentish Town, we stop at the shop and Crilly buys me a carton of food: soup and cheese and biscuits and cereal, chocolate and bread and ham and whatever else takes my fancy. I follow him down the aisle and throw random packages into the basket. He lets me. He follows.

Crilly has tidied the flat, and my bed is made up for a queen with extra duvets and fluffy pillows. Cat O'Fun rubs up against my legs. Anita makes a pot of tea for the three of us.

It is then that I spot the post. Two bills and a threatening letter about a parking ticket. It ends with a note from the bailiffs, saying that they will be around to collect compensation if the bill is not paid. It has been forwarded from my previous address and it is well out of date. I read the return address and put on my coat.

'I must go to Holloway,' I say. Crilly and Anita are suitably perplexed. They do not stir. 'I must go to Holloway,' I repeat. 'The office is there. The bailiffs will be around. I'm going to Holloway . . .'

Anita pours out the tea. 'They won't be around today, Claudia. They probably won't be around at all. Just send a cheque explaining that you only just got the letter.'

'I don't have any envelopes,' I say, pacing about the room. The fact that I do not have envelopes causes me physical pain. 'It may be too late for a cheque by post. They'll take everything.' The thought of being without my VCR, my television and my records is more horrible than anything.

'They won't come,' Anita counters calmly. 'Not after a month. And it isn't much of a bill.'

'What the fuck do you know about it?' I hiss. 'There may be more bills at the old flat!' The cat, who is hungry, follows me in circles. Anita is silent. Crilly rises to placate me. He puts his hands on my shoulders. I could scream, 'Piss off you paddy wanker,' but instead I sit.

'They won't come,' he says. 'Not so soon. Not over a trifle. They only do that to scare you. Now get to bed; you should be in bed.'

I bury my face in my knees. I know they are right. I am defeated. Anita hands me my tea and leaves. I complain about her. I say she thinks she's got it together just because she's American. Crilly reminds me that I'm American too, and just because I know a few words of British slang, I shouldn't be getting airs about myself. His lecture is comforting. He puts me to bed. I ask him to lie beside me. He does. I tell him I can't sleep. He says to close my eyes and rest quietly; sleep will come.

'Crilly,' I say as we lie together, 'when the nurse gave me the anaesthetic, she jabbed me so deep that I could feel it throbbing in my veins like an explosion, and it hurt like anything. Did you ever feel it like that — the needle, I mean?'

Crilly wraps his arms around my waist.

'Every now and then,' he says, 'but that's the best part.' He kisses me.

'Funny,' I reply. 'I thought I would fucking die.'

We sleep.

When I awake, it is well past three. Crilly has gone and there is a sheet of cardboard beside me on the pillow. 'Gone to the shops for you,' it reads. I sit up and stretch. I wonder how long he will be. I know he hasn't really gone to the shops. I turn on the television. A woman with a stupid wedged haircut is selling deodorant.

'Shove it up your armpit!' I yell, and collapse into a fit of giggles. I decide to go out for cigarettes; a short walk will do me good. I put on my coat and leave. I walk to the newsagent. It isn't far. I feel okay. I am not sore.

The newsagent is crowded, full of schoolchildren in uniform. They make a great clamour; they take their time, just making noise. They seem so brittle they terrify me. I keep thinking one of them will shove me in the ribs, or tell me that I'm ugly. I wait awhile, until they have all been seen to. I am about to pay when I realise I brought no money. I leave. My legs are heavy. I think of the gym; I wonder how I ever could have been there. I wonder how anybody could ever go to gyms. The sky is grey and abysmal; it has grown blacker since morning. I hate it. We are in the dead of winter—sooty blackness falls by four in the afternoon. I pass more schoolchildren. I hate them as well. I start running, but my body puts up a fight. How I hate my body!

When I get home, Crilly is there. He has turned on the lights, the heat and the television. He is making pancakes. 'I hate them all,' I say tearfully.

'What?' He comes and helps me off with my coat. I collapse on the floor. He follows me down and holds me in his arms.

'You're shivering,' he says, and carries me back to bed. He tells me to relax and watch television. He scolds me for leaving the flat. He puts the lavender neon on. He fetches the silver foil.

We sit together in bed. Crilly makes a silver tube and puts it in my hand. He lights the match below the brown patch and I suck in and follow the smoke.

'Hold it in,' he advises, 'as long as you can.' He watches as I hold it in. When I cannot hold it any longer, I blow the smoke into his mouth. We stay kissing for a bit. When I pull away, I feel fantastic. Lit from the inside, dripping with light. We embark on a second burn. I love the shiny brown line, I love the crinkle of the silver foil. Crilly turns off the telly and puts on a Billie Holiday record. I love her. I love her more than anything. He knows it.

'It's like Christmas,' I say to him. He caresses me. I stroke his hair.

'Don't be sad,' I say, 'everything is all right now.' He gives me another burn and he has one for himself, blowing the smoke back into my mouth afterwards. I flash on something but I can't think what it is; something empty, something white. I start to speak, but I do not want to lose the smoke. I hold it again, enjoying the tension in my bosom as I do. He watches me. I forget about the flash of white. I release the smoke into the air.

'I love you,' he says. We make love. I am not permitted to have intercourse for three weeks after surgery, but there are other things we can do and we do them. Technical things do not matter. Behind closed eyes, I think: we're fused, Crilly and me, just fused, like euphoria, eu-fuse-ia.

And the hole is full of him, his consuming fleshy self. I am his and his alone. It rains outside. I float and how I love to fuck.

There are tears on his face and I wipe them away. He is beautiful. He holds me like the devil himself. I love the sound his bracelet makes.

Soon, my breasts are hard and lumpy and lactose dribbles from them. I have been told that this might happen. Crilly does not mind. He kisses them and licks the milk from his lips. Giving milk seems funny; it makes me laugh and then cry in a stoned, sleepy, dribbly way. Crilly does the same. We make love for hours and hours, long into the night, and I am not afraid.

the ladies' pond

The bleakness of my street in winter overwhelms me, though it is a pretty street on an uphill slope with a row of terraced houses on either side. In the summertime, it is alive with hot fumes and rampant dogs and fashionable bathers crawling up Highgate Road on their way to the Heath, where they claim respective ponds and languor till the sky slowly turns to a soothing summer gold. In these months twilight never comes before half past eight or nine o'clock. And the bathers leave on foot or in jeeps or bikes or minis.

The summer is a hot one. According to *The Independent*, our temperatures are Mediterranean. I frequent the Heath, the Ladies' Pond, where I meet Kelly and Jo and lush Simone, sunning themselves in topless array and munching on nectarines which drip down necks and towels. One day, I bring black cherries.

Topless and nude, ladies are strewn in abundance on a hilly grass beach and in the sunken leaves below the lifeguard. Ladies swim in the pond itself, which is crisp and clean with ducks upon it. Ladies sunbathe in convival clusters upon a generous wooden float. I chase the ducks, paddling after them in the water, though I am a grown woman and topless like everybody else. The lifeguard, who weighs fifteen stone and does not shave beneath her arms, yells at me to stop. I stop.

The first time I visit the Ladies' Pond, I exclaim to Kelly, 'It's like a Fellini film,' to which she says in a lazy Scottish brogue,

'Perhaps . . . I don't know . . . I canny recall him to mind just noo.' I do not elaborate but take my place on a towel with the others.

When I am asked to think of a happy London, I think of this place in July and of my lazy pondmates: Kelly and Simone and Jo, the acidhouse DJ. I think of the eclectic women on baby blankets, bare beside picnic baskets and one another, pleased to be sated by nothing more than a book and a cigarette, a glass of cider and a chat or a piece of quiche, meatless, of course. Butch tattooed women survey the hedges for Peeping Toms. There are white, black and Asian lovers; the lovers are largely nude. There are professionals feasting on rare weekday picnics of wine and poultry and biscuits. There are long-haired, weather-beaten hippies, short-haired sprightly trendies, socialists and socialites, feminists and Highgate wives, and the women who are both. There are women of relaxed obesity, and sylph-like creatures with firm and boyish bodies. One time, I meet a girl whose name I don't remember. She studies theology at Edinburgh. She tells me she has been to every temple on the Greek islands of Mykonos and Santorini. She is clever but her voice is soft and stupid like syrup. She has no ear for irony. I do not introduce her to my other friends.

Kelly is the sweetest thing I have ever seen, with a face like Raggedy Ann and ginger dreadlocks. She is small and slight. Her girlfriend, Josephine, does not take to the water, so Kelly and I go in alone with Simone, treading in unison till the chill is mellowed, and swim to the deep end where we cling to the buoy and discuss other people. Simone is cheered by the Ladies' Pond, and in the course of summer she drinks less and dyes her hair a platinum blonde and tans herself till her eyes shine. She forgets about her absent man. Wet and splattering to keep warm, we giggle too much while small crowish birds squawk strange somethings in the swamp bit. We are not maudlin.

Crilly does not feel alienated by my visits to the Heath, though he confesses to missing me by day and he is usually at home when I return. He likes my sticky, sweaty body which smells of nectarine and baby oil and a spliff that Jo has rolled beneath a shadowy cove of eucalyptus. I enjoy the heat of his hands.

Most summer afternoons, Crilly will have scored. We sit upon our bed with a roll of foil, several bars of chocolate and the hardback edition of a Georgia O'Keeffe retrospective (nicked from Dillons) upon which he lays a tube and a neat square of foil flattened by his own deft fingers and the gear itself in its cosy half-inch envelope. I hold my breath until it is melted, for fear it will fly away. Taking the same precaution, he melts it quickly and carefully, acutely aware of rare summer breezes or the compulsion to sneeze. And he blows the smoke back into my mouth. I take the tube in my hand while he lights the foil from underneath. His movement is steady and I admire him for it. I learn how to follow just a split-second behind him. Together, we make a smooth dry track upon the silver.

Unbathed and weary from the bake of the sun and the refreshment of cool water, I am delicious with the skag inside my chest and the sweet, smoky aroma surrounding me, and the touch of my lover and his hot arms about my waist, and his words:

'. . . Hold it in flower, don't let it escape. Hold it, hold fast . . .'

We linger before the telly and finish the pack and hold one another while dusk filters through the blinds, the silver blinds which are always shut. We wait, as darkness falls, in the hollow of my home.

maggie delaney

Maggie Delaney is a lightly freckled, chocolate-haired, blue-eyed thing from the waterside Irish town of Malahide. The first time I meet her, I wear an unflattering dress. Unlike Crilly, she speaks in a clear and Anglicised accent and, more than once, I have heard her criticised by her countrymen for not taking pride in her own. I don't know whether she does or not. Crilly says that if you listen well, you can hear the Irish in her right enough. She shows it in temper, and when she is ill. Crilly would know; he was her lover for three years, before he was mine. They remain friends, though she is quick to be petulant over telephone messages left unanswered and favours left undone. But she calls him a friend, and I have no objections. Not at first.

I meet her, in my unflattering dress, at the Warrior one muggy Saturday. I am with my mother, stepfather and half brother who are in London for a week. I show them the Camden Market, and my brother, Winchell, buys an old, funereal coat by the Lock, while I stand by and smoke spliffs with the bootleg sellers in bright berets. In his coat, Winchell looks like a Dickensian undertaker; he embarrasses me. Still, he wears it proudly, despite the warm weather and his age of only eleven, and who am I to deprive him of his girth, his boorish style, his fun? We are heavy with packages. My folks want to see the inside of a real pub. I take them to the Warrior.

The beer garden is an urban embarrassment of grey pebble beach and picnic tables. We sit there. Empty cans and bottles litter the turf and make crunching sounds like oyster shells when they are stepped on. A clothes-line hangs between two high windows, hovering above like a tawdry hammock from the sky. Larry, my stepfather, sits stiffly with a pained expression on his face. A bearded vagrant with mucky skin and deep-socketed eyes tries to annoy him. He croons a slurred and cheerful chain of obscenities: 'fancy a grind my luv'. He won't go. We retreat to the inside, where marketers and pinstriped shirts from TV-AM suck on Saturday Specials. Guinness and Beamish and whiskey and lime. The Warrior is crowded. By a stroke of fortune, we find a rickety table to sit at. The vagrant follows us in, grinning toothlessly at Larry, saliva dribbling from his purple lips. He is barred by the manager. It is a sunny autumn day. Beyond the open window frame where the glass has been lifted, the sky is splendid. My mother comments on what a fine afternoon it is. Though she is an American tourist, she looks elegant in her high Italian boots and I think, I can always know my mother by the briskness of her gait and the suede upon her feet. My mother swings her legs beneath the table.

From the bar, I spot Crilly in a corner in the back room. He beckons me over and introduces me to Maggie. There are no audible words between us. She averts her eyes and pricks the tear in her tights with one incisive nail.

I will always remember what she looks like. She is wet with elegant reserve. She nurses a vodka and orange and sits still with long stockinged legs turned inwardly but not awkwardly. She wears a black cocktail dress — the sort they wear in Soho at art school gatherings in flats white and minimal. (I know those flats: copies of *iD* magazine on the one table, drinking something gold against whitewashed walls, snaking lines of speed in the loo with the cracked mirror.) Maggie's eyes are long and wide like certain nuts, and they turn up at the ends like maidens from Disney. Her hair is short and black. She brings to my mind something chic and continuous, like an Italic. I didn't know she would be so attractive. She makes me nervous. Crilly tries to coax me into the booth but I shrug out from under his arms and make an excuse about the family. Appallingly on cue, Winchell approaches us, fat and gnome-like and swimming in his new-old coat. Crilly hugs my brother back warmly and introduces him to the languid one. She nods her head. I want to retreat to the opposite end of the room. I hate my skirt; it has pale flowers on it. I crave the safety of a tabletop and a Bloody Mary rich with pulp. Sensing the chill in me, Crilly eases me to the jukebox and presses a small bottle into my hand. Winchell stands eager and forgotten several feet away. 'You wanted it,' says Crilly. I take the methadone and hold it fast in my pocket. I narrow my eyes to stare into his; the light of the pub is dim as dust and I cannot make out the pinpoints. Yet I detect the glare of glass in the emerald bit. He kisses me. He smells sweetly of sulphur. 'I'll be round at seven,' he says, and I know he means nine. I kiss him back. I now have two things to look forward to.

The bottle of green snug in my jacket, I return to my family. Winchell follows. I glance behind to catch Maggie's eyes. She does not register the gesture, but I can feel her watching as we go.

Bad Billy McGregor, from Aberdeen, is talking to my stepfather. He is telling Larry about his whippets. I knew him once, I knew the whippets. He was the sort of man who'd turn up only when he said he wouldn't. He ran, often, up the Heath with the whippets, in the deadest night. He loves fast skinny dogs and sulphate, driving drunk in someone else's car and sprawling, comatose, Saturday reprieves, watching the football. His eyes are never still. He made an attempt on Crilly's life with a pocket knife once; but now they speak amicably to one another, they just don't seem to remember. It is only me who remembers. Billy smells of stout and talc, and his voice is like the scrape of something feral on a smooth steel pan.

'Still shaftin' the paddy?' he asks.

'Yes, thank you,' I say.

Maggie is drawing close to the bar. She does not look my way. I move in closer to Billy. Does she know Billy? Has she met him in the Three Pigeons? Does Billy find her attractive? She orders a cloudy greenish drink with ice cubes. She walks tall and straight, a little stiff. The barman hands her a second drink, a Tennents. That will be for Crilly. As Maggie turns, I catch a flash of eye, fairy blue but just a bit milky. I wonder if she has used with Crilly today. I wonder if one day Maggie and Crilly and I will use together.

Billy recognises Larry from a detective show.

'Tha was magic when you jus bashed th' fat guy to fock,' he says.

'Yes,' says Larry. He exchanges a glance with my mother. I squeeze the bottle in my pocket, making certain it is there. I think of dashing off to the loo to drink it but I decide to wait. The dribbling vagrant appears like a wayward soldier in the open window frame. My mother laughs loudly. Billy delivers a tirade of appreciation and Larry, sitting tightly with his brow creased, doesn't understand a word.

strung out

I have been back with Crilly for a month now, or two. I sit alone one Sunday evening at the Old Ship, waiting. At the next booth are three junkies, nursing pints of Guinness. One of them, a bearded beer-bellied fellow in a tank top and tattoos, approaches.

'You Crilly's bird?" he asks.

'In a way.'

'You seen him?'

'Why?'

'Well he said he'd be in.'

'Why?'

'We've been waiting. You know.'

'He isn't dealing.'

'I know that. But he's helping us out.'

'Oh? Who?'

He gestures to his friends. 'Me and some mates. Johnny. Terry. Mick.' I look at Johnny, Terry and Mick, and I decide that I hate them.

'Who else?'

'That's all.'

'Well, I don't know where he is.'

'You seen Maggie?'

'Not recently.'

He returns to his table. I am lying. I am expecting Crilly and he is late. Perry walks through the door, wearing a tall trenchcoat. I sit erect. I am happy to see him. I feel a stirring in my loins. I call to him. He turns and sits beside me.

'How's it goin?' His voice is deep and Dublin, like Crilly's, but unlike Crilly, his words are sparse. His black hair sticks out from wind and rain. He is such a handsome man and I know he will make us happy.

'Weird, Perry. I feel like shit.'

'Don't I fockin' know it. Have you seen Crilly?'

Something about his stance, so fidgety and uneasy, makes my heart sink. Desire leaves my body and I am forlorn and full of hate. I want to say, you stupid skinny Mick, why are you asking me?

'Not yet. Is anything happening tonight? Can't you help us?'

Perry shakes his head. His eyes unusually wide. Being clean doesn't suit him. I want to tell him so.

'It's a slow night, darlin'. Where's your man?'

'I don't know, Perry. Is Crilly the only one with any information round here?'

'No, but Jane got fockin' stood up, and there's a rumour that Van might have something, but he won't serve fock all people. He likes Crilly. I reckon Crilly might have a better chance.'

'What about you?'

'Nothin'.'

'Shit!'

'I know.'

My stomach is churning. Perry offers to buy me a drink, but I will not give him the satisfaction. My innards are stiff and metallic, like broken machinery. The smell of booze is making me nauseous. Perry's fags lay half out of their packet on the table, but I do not want to smoke. I hate cigarettes anyway, what's the point? Sticks of nothing in your gob. White rods the shimmery sheen of birdshit. That queasy asthmatic sensation in your chest, all that smoke and nothing, nothing but smoke. Just smoke.

Maggie comes into the pub, her hair wet and pulled back from her face. She wears jeans and a tatty jumper. I have never seen her looking so sick and skinny. She makes a beeline for Perry. I know she will be disappointed, and this gives me satisfaction. Her eyes, also, are huge with unwitting cleaniless. I don't care. I pity no man, I pity no woman, I pity no dog. She shakes. Following a stint of desperate rhetoric with Perry, she turns to me. 'Claudia,' she says loudly, 'have you got 10p I can borrow?'

I want to say no but I don't and I throw her a coin, aiming for her gut. She takes it and makes for the phone box. Perry looks at me and looks away, his eyes darting everywhere. I follow his eyes from the bar to the jukebox, to the bearded one, to two like-faced girls with stocky builds and bleached blonde hair. They are also waiting.

Crilly bursts into the pub. I can tell by his face that he has not been successful. He is stopped at the door by an emaciated woman with a grotesque burn injury, whom I have not seen before. Poor ugly cow, a lot of good her waiting will do. He speaks hastily to her and flies to our table, where he does not sit but squats in front of me.

'No joy,' he says.

Perry, who has heard, stubs his cigarette and swears. I want to weep. I swallow and speak in a tremor. I try to be gracious. 'What about Agar Grove?' My voice is high and desperate.

'No.'

'Caversham Road?'

'Nothing.'

'Why not?'

'Because there's nothing, Claudia!'

'Why the hell not? I feel like I'm fucking gonna —'

'How the fock do you think I feel? I'm the one running

around in the fockin' rain!'

'But I'm paying for it, this time!'

'You're not. You're not payin' for nothing!'

'Stop saying "nothing"!'

'Look at you. You're sounding like a fockin' junkie!'

'Well . . .'

Maggie approaches, hovering at Crilly's shoulder.

'You can save your breath!' I snap at her. She ignores me, whining about how he was supposed to meet her at the Bullet's Head. Her voice is shrill and agitated. Like mine, but Irish, as English affectation slips away. I consider telling her to speak properly, just for spite.

'Both of youse, just hold onto yourselves for a second. Just hold on.'

Crilly wants to hold it together. He crosses the room. He speaks with the similar looking stocky girls. I watch hopefully. After a moment, Perry rises to join him. Maggie sits in Perry's seat, not meeting my eyes, sweating. The jukebox is playing 'Ricky Don't Lose that Number', and it reminds me of carpools in the seventh grade. I take a deep breath and try to calm myself, to still the noisy, rusty jagged parts. I think I'm bleeding on the inside. After ten slow minutes, Crilly returns.

'There might be something in Prince of Wales Road.'

'Who?'

'A Welsh guy called Richard. Don't get your hopes up.'

But my hopes are up and rising. Crilly tells me to meet him at the Hope and Vixen in half an hour. He rides off on the bicycle, my bicycle, which is too small for him. Perry stays behind to use the phone. Maggie, who is dubious of the Prince of Wales connection, leaves in pursuit of something better. I drive to the Hope in my ugly, crusty car which makes horrible squeaking sounds in the rain.

At the Hope, an Irish band called Mo and McNamara are

playing live upon a modest stage. I order a vodka and orange and sit in a corner beneath peeling mauve and silver flock wallpaper. The pub, usually packed full of young Camden locals, old men from Winterbottom's Home for the Vagrant and Elderly and crusaders from south of the river, is nearly empty tonight. Several ancient men in worn and baggy clothes sit at separate tables drinking neat whiskey and half pints of Beamish. The Hope smells not only of beer but of new sawdust, cheese and onion crisps, and mildew. At a table crammed into the wall, I stare into space, trying to ignore an old man who yells at the barmaid and another who sits doubled over with his pink mottled head against the table, sleeping and snoring. The band is made up of two men. One is old with a shadowy face and long black hair, and the other is younger and pudgy, with a pale cherubic face and narrow green eyes. He sings. His voice is not bad; in fact it is rather lovely, like the lead vocalist of The Chieftains. I try to listen. Though my stomach is ruptured like a crushed tube of tomato puree, I manage to hear some of the words.

> On Raglan Road
> on an autumn day
> I saw her first, and knew
> That her dark hair would weave a snare
> that I would one day rue
> I saw the danger, then I walked
> along the enchanted way
> And I said let grief
> be a falling leaf
> At the dawning of the day . . .

I gulp down the orange drink and order another one. I consider moving to Ireland and marrying a road worker in Kerry. I will produce many children and get fat and wear stretch maternity jeans (even after I have given birth) and an apron with a daisy on it. I will drink on my own and listen to the Dubliners. I finish my drink. Keep your mind free, I am telling myself. Keep it clear. Breathe deeply. Don't feel the pain, the rust. I return to my table and try to listen . . .

> On Grafton Street in November
> We tripped lightly along the ledge . . .

But I cannot.

By the time the first bell rings, I have waited an hour. The sleeping man is still asleep and the other has left. A big-built Scottish woman, who has been playing pool in the other section of the pub, crosses over to the east side of the bar and puts in her last orders. I know the woman. She is called Josie; she used to visit my flat with her boyfriend, to stage violent, public rows. Once she stuffed her diaphragm into one of my neon lights, breaking it, shattering it. I pray that she will not see me now. She doesn't. I think, maybe if God has answered that trivial prayer, he will also answer my monumental ones. Maybe it is good that Crilly has not arrived. He has probably found some awkward connection on the other side of town, south of the river, where reggae blares, and they won't cut it with too much sugar . . .

When Josie has gone, I stand, unsteady, and buy another vodka, neat, thinking, fuckall good this will do. I pour it into the remainder of my old drink, so that it still tastes faintly of orange juice. Like a small child unwedded to booze, I don't like the taste of it; I like sweet things, like Dr Pepper and root beer, and white chocolate animals from Woolworth's. I drink fast. I am not drunk so much as queasy. My nausea has not left me. I shiver. I am nothing but a stomach of cheap tin, empty but for the clanking of a few tin cans which have been squashed by a gargantuan hand and thrown together. They are ruthless, those squashed and empty cans. The audience, sparse and sad, do not call for an encore, but Mo and McNamara embark upon a lonely farewell tune just the same. I admire them. Their arrangement is simple. The older man plays an accordion, and the younger one plays a tin whistle in the musical interlude. They sing a Pogues song.

> One summer evening drunk to hell
> I sat there nearly lifeless . . .
> An old man in the corner sang
> Where the water lilies grow
> And on the jukebox, Johnny sang
> about a thing called love
> And it's how're ya kid
> and what's your name
> and how'd you bloody know . . .

I know the song well. In fact I love it. I have loved it for years. I try to feel it now, to let it crawl inside of me, to replace my sickness with sweet, melodic grief. I want to lie in a sunny green field. I want to weep the tears of dying soldiers and widowed mothers. I want to hold something deep and soft beneath the flesh, something as easy and fluid as nostalgia (as tangible as a stuffed bear), as simple as a final lullaby, lulling me to softness, lulling me to sleep. I want to hear the country rain on the roof of our house, where Daddy read to me from *Where the Wild Things Are*. I try, try hard, to feel it. But I cannot, for that which is sick is strong. It holds on and keeps the gentle tears away.

On the other side of the pub, Perry scurries through the door. I can see him through the open bar. He does not acknowledge me. He sits behind a half-screen, perusing the faces of customers as they amble away, their arms full of cans for the road. When he has not seen the man he has hoped to see, his long spine slackens and he falls back upon the red vinyl of the booth with his eyes closed and his foot shaking in a livid tic. One old, old man, drunk and limp as old laundry but standing, yells at another old man who is sleeping with his head on the table. 'Jack, where's that fuckin' fiver you owe me?' The sleeping man does not wake.

I leave the Hope and drive home. I check the answerphone.

'I'm out here in Walthamstow . . . Jez . . . I'm fockin' soaked. I think we're out of luck.'

I crawl into my bed and crouch in a foetal position, a pillow stuffed between my knees and chest. The room is dark, but passing cars cast yellowy shadows upon the wall. I try to sleep but I can only doze, and I am frequently aware of a pulse, a rattle, a rustiness rippling through me. In my bed is a faint smell of excrement. At three a.m. Crilly comes home, wet and defeated. He reaches for me and holds me tight, and the tremble of him is tremendous. I can't stand the weight of him. I pull away.

'You better not hold me,' I say to him. My skin hurts. Crilly turns over and lies with his back stiff and petulant. The sounds of the night are low. I hear the West Indian boys swearing and yelling at one another in quick, hoarse voices. I hear the thump of the cat flap as Cat O'Fun tumbles through it without the feline grace of his fellows. I shake. Sounds are no longer sounds to me. They are scrapes and sores, mockers of failure, players in a relentless team of agitation. I am not the same as I was before. Not the same as I ever was. I do not sleep.

nantucket

We went to Nantucket. My father and I, and sometimes my mother. Every summer. We rented a tawny triangle of a house that smelled of sweet musty oak and Coppertone suntan oil and Bordeaux biscuits. (In later years, adult years, while sitting in London stuffed with wholemeal digestives soaked in tea, I would be filled with the wheat and candour of this smell, and I would hold the digestive as long as I could in my mouth, as if aiming to grasp its exact ingredient and texture, to become its body and its recipe). The house was built by a local architect called Cecil, an old man with a raspy white beard, who'd lost half an arm to a wayward chainsaw. The house was set beside a wood. In the wood, Cecil had carved into a tree trunk a small swing for a child that had since grown and died in Vietnam. I took the swing for my own, and revelled in its leafy solitude and the soft pungent moss which grew beneath it, carpeting a pillowy clump of earth. Also secluded in the forest stood a platform of marble. It was for nothing but to counter the parallel sky, and I found it mystical in its impracticality. I took a box of Lego to the slab and built cities of red, white and black until the cool white surface grew scarce beneath me and my concoctions. The first time we rented the house, I was three. My mother and father were married, though never in the same room together. It seemed, in fact, that Cecil's house belonged to my father, who made a cave for himself out of its damp and its wood, the sweet musk of its corners. He was busy, my father, with unfinished canvases from

art school, generous manuscripts about Beethoven and
Medieval painters, a manual typewriter snug enough to fit upon
a window ledge, and soup bowls heaped with cheddar cheese
goldfish, gently serenaded by an old electric fan as I, in my turn,
busied myself with Lego upon that slab of perfect marble. Mom
was a visitor. She came through on weekends, the smirk of the
city still upon her face, wearing opal rings always cool to the
touch, and highly glossed lips of mauve. She was like a cube of
chrome, sleek and symmetrical. She was the Amtrak commuter
line that one never catches. She packed Rolling Stones and Ray
Charles into a leather case, along with a tiny bottle of Chanel
and a selected volume of Beat poetry, and she came to us.
Daddy's hairline was receding. He wore simple plaid shirts and
corduroys, even in summer. He sat at a makeshift desk of
unfinished lumber, and wrote and played with his thinning hair.
Occasionally he produced a camera and pointed it at me, as I
played on the lawn with my limber chestnut friend, Katrina
(who would later drop out of high school and become a porno
star in Paris), or at me alone, mainly alone. Our favourite photo
was taken of me on the marble slab. I was slight and crew-cutted,
surrounded by tiny plastic wheels. I was trying to build a car. I
knew the names of all the cars. Daddy taught them to me. In the
city, I stood at the window and identified the cars as they
breezed by. I also knew all of the states and their capitals. Later,
in my teens, I would forget. But then, I knew. At night, Daddy
read to me, and though I had many books, there were only four I
wished to hear. The first two were *Where the Wild Things Are*
and *In the Night Kitchen* by Maurice Sendak, ornate with
fabulous wide-mouthed forest monsters and small plump boys
fallling through the night devoured by dough. The third was
Babar, though we always skipped the part where Babar's mother
is shot by the hunter, and the fourth was a sing-a-long story
called *The Fox Went Out on a Chilly Night*. We sang along.

> O, the Fox went out on a chilly night
> and he prayed to the moon to give him light . . .

My mother had a bicycle with a childseat. Once or twice, we rode to the beach. We stopped at the farmers' market for cheese and grapes. I sat in the back of her bicycle. She rode quickly, pausing only for traffic (which was scarce) or bumps in the road. I did like the smells; drifts of Johnson's baby shampoo wafting from her hair and mine, the beachy, balmy smell in my face as we ascended Elderberry Road, that persevering odour of fresh tar and suntan oil. Gaining the tar-sweated hill with my mother's lean legs pumping swiftly, the willowy sight of streaky high dunes on the horizon awaited us, waving to and fro as they did, sheltering an occasional beige box of a house, a modern cube. My mother told me about the famous people who lived in them. She knew some of them. My mother's hair was fine and straight then, falling easily down her back. No matter how often she sunbathed, her skin was always very white. In contrast, I was like my father, and I darkened rapidly in the sun until I was nearly the shade of terracotta.

We left the beach at around six. My mother told me it was six; I could not feel the lateness in the day, other than the westward blare of a reluctantly falling sun. Soaked with it and languid from the heat, with the scent of salt and sand still heavy in my nose, I asked if we could stop at the high slope of grass off Elderberry Road. My mother parked her bicycle in the shoulder and took my hand, and we climbed to the top of the hill. We lay on the brink of its descent and rolled quickly downwards, our faces full of earth and grass one instant and then rotating madly and finally up to the brazen blue sky leaking through the trees. My mother giggled all the way down. We climbed up again and rolled down a second time, Mom sighing and giggling again, again. Her laugh was always the same; high and birdlike, very young. It was wonderful to roll; that first second push off, sluggish with the anticipation of falling, that moment of tumbling when all was forgotten but frenetic strips of blue light and blades of green in our skin and clothes, and that next to last stretch when we knew we'd roll forever (or at least well into the shoulder of the road), and that final jolt and halt, nearly violent, as the bottom was reached. Once there, we lifted ourselves and looked at one another, both of us laughing, trudging grass-stained to the top again. More powerful even than the scent of newly-mowed grass or flickering glimpses of sky was the scent of my mother in her peach halter, her back slender and white, and the forever-ish trickly sound of her high giggle, the giggle of delight and fresh sloping green hills.

the cow's lip

Gemma wants to do something different on a Friday night. So do I. We complain loudly about cliques at smoky Camden locals; the Devonshire Arms, the Bull and Gate, the Hen and Gentleman. The names of familiar pubs exhaust me. We consider bowling in Streatham. We consider bingo in Plaistow. Fringe theatre in Islington is too bourgeois. Art exhibitions are too familiar; we are sure to run into a person we know — Slow Bill, angular Adam, a friend of a friend or somebody's ex. We have been to clubs, those dancing tornedoes, those ricocheting bodies under mad silver strobes, those siren samples, those scratch mixes, 'CAN YOU FEEL IT?!' crying over and over again.

Mind, I do like the girls I don't know in the ladies' room, gelling knives of black hair and saying, 'He's a cunt, that one.' I like the clubs when it's time to leave.

We are weary of Acidhouse and Warehouses and Ron's living-rooms; the plastic Cindy dolls upon the wall, the anaemic cat in people's laps, the dope and the drivel.

We pile into the car as if embarking on a real motor trip; Gemma and I are in front, Anita in the back. Anita is content to let us decide.

I have always felt a proclivity for Kilburn. I like to shop on the Kilburn High Road. I like the wide-hipped, grey-bobbed mothers with skin like old stucco, yelling in aggressive Cork accents to small, over-bundled children; I enjoy the tribes of

weird and underfed adolescents, swearing deeply in hoarse
Donegal brogues, toting large bottles of cider and smooth
Kerrygold butter for their mums. I can tell, by the dialects,
which part of Ireland the shoppers hail from; I have wilfully
acquired a skill for accents. And there are tinkers; grubby,
potato-faced, carrot-haired children, running through the
aisles, lifting packets of Smarties and banana cake.

Tonight, we are urban tourists; trespassers. We are almost an
affront, flamboyant voyeurs. Anita wears a Tibetan scarf and
high grey leg-warmers, her hair a tumble of untamed curls.
Gemma is glamorous as always, her lips a large pucker of blood
red, her hair a shock of bleached white-blonde, her legs fish-
netted and mini-skirted, high Doc Martens on her feet. I wear
black. My hair is platinum, like Gemma's but shorter, finger-
curled. If I had the courage to grow out my hair and take on the
streets without frill or face paint, bangles or heels and all such
accessories of fear and vanity, then I would be seen far less and
see much more. But I have no such courage. It is not enough for
me to explore, to retreat graciously into the dust and floorboards of those exotic places. I have to be noticed, appeased or
approved of. And yet, I know that I am cheating.

I settle on a place called the Cow's Lip. It is a corner pub with
two entrances, painted red. In front stands a group of Irish
Countrymen (Culteys Crilly calls them) wearing faded caps of
rust and plaid, holding pints of Guinness to their chests.

The first thing that catches my eye is the mural. Painted
directly upon the wall, it takes up almost the entire pub. It is an
ambling Irish field painted in broad, sweeping shades of green; a
rich green for the trees, a lighter green for the grass. A farmer
bearing a sack toils in the field, his martyred face half blocked by
his cap, a sedentary cow in his tow. The sky is of a rich sea blue
that is almost grotesque in its fullness of colour, broken only by
an indignant stream of clouds piping up in the distant horizon.

In one corner, a tired traveller plays the flute beneath a willow tree, his cheese and ale spread out before him on a handkerchief. Gemma, who is an art student, gapes at the mural.

'How awful,' she says.

'Shut up,' I say.

'I mean, it's so awful it's wonderful.'

Gemma is stark in the middle of the crowd, her shoulders slightly stooped. I oughtn't snap, I think. I buy drinks for her and Anita and myself. Anita orders a Guinness and I am proud of her.

The Cow's Lip is divided into two parts; the front has the mural and stage, and a pool table off to the right, and several scattered booths stuffed with groups of locals who seem to have grown from their tough wood benches, like the clustered branches of an ancient, overgrown tree. They hover together in their crowded safety, their tables littered by empty pint glasses rimmed and dripping with the foamy froth of leftover lager, and ashtrays overflowing like untidy clumps of ashen moss. The locals are men and women, generally older, their bloated flesh spilling histories of things I do not know. To the right there are darts; the dartmen and their flooding flannel trousers, stooped and intent. I have seen it all in my very own Camden often enough, but it is new to me somehow. Perhaps the mural makes it new, so shamelessly bright upon the wall like something spilt, and the restless assortment of weekend patrons who watch the stage with agitated and expectant eyes. I wonder what they are watching for. The musicians are innocuous enough; three middle-aged Irishmen with somber and kindly red faces, playing gentle Irish tunes, meeting only the faces of one another. When Gemma speaks, a woman flinches. I see her. A lank-haired, wild-eyed, ageless woman with a body like wire and a shapeless tunic. I think she is very beautiful. Gemma suggests we go to the back.

But I refuse. We stand in the clearing amongst the watchful

eyes, the listless, standing bodies, still sober and milling about us. In the event of a fire, we could not make our way out. This brings to me a strange solace. The crowd clears. I see people who look very young, clad solidly in khaki; the girls in khaki dresses, their costumes tidy and generic like girl scout uniforms. They wear straps across their chests and square caps. One girl cannot be more than twelve. She holds a drum.

All at once, we are surrounded by men.

'Where are you coming from tonight?'

'Camden.'

'And before that?'

'America.'

'Where in America?'

'Los Angeles. But I was born in New York.'

'Ah, the East. Well.'

Gemma is not so fortunate, being a Londoner. But she is so pretty, they forgive her for it. Anita keeps her mouth shut, and lets the lads gaze at her fine dark features which have the look of something ethnic about them. I am enjoying my own attention; a carpenter in a large mustard sweater, and a sweet-faced young lad with glasses. He knew Bobby Sands. He knew Frances Hughes. He tells me about them.

The band is good. They play 'The Green Fields of France' and 'Carrickfergus' and 'Don't Forget Your Shovel if You Want to Go To Work'. As patrons pour into the pub, the band becomes louder. Our suitors have to shout just to get our names. But I am tired of my voice, I want to watch the band. The khaki scouts sprout in number, appearing from nowhere. They do not only make their way through stuffed and clamoring doorways, but emerge from the unseen bowels of the pub, as though they have held themselves privately for days in the cellar, waiting with bated breath, presenting themselves only as the hour grows ripe. There are more drums. And flutes. And whistles, not played but held snugly in their arms, like babies. Between each song, a chant pushes up like a hushed inhale, murmuring from a hesitant corner. The scouts lead.

'The Brets. The Brets. The Brets oot noo.'

I turn to the carpenter. 'They have Scottish accents.'

'Aye.'

'But why? You're all Irish, aren't you?'

'I'm from County Clare meself. But you'll be finding quite a few of the Scots in here tonight.'

'Really?'

The carpenter nods. He is pleased by my ignorance. The chant starts again. Louder, this time.

'The Brets. The Brets. The Brets oot noo!'

By this time, the pub is so stuffed with people that I daren't take a deep breath. I am hot. I take off my jumper and stand in my tank top, sipping a whiskey I have been bought. On the stage, the Scottish scouts form an even row behind the three piece band. One boy, a child, begins a steady drum roll. And then a drum march. Loud. Scouts of both sexes begin to march, in place.

Tookatookatook. Tickatickatick. Tookatookatookatookatoo-katookatook . . .

Anita is enthralled. She speaks.

'Is today some kind of holiday?' she asks sensibly.

'In a way,' replies a striking young man of white, white skin, black hair, black eyes (black Irish and he's lovely). 'Today is the anniversary of the Derry slaying '72. Bloody Sunday. Today is the anniversary of Bloody Sunday.'

And now for the march. I caress my naked shoulders. One of the scouts, a woman, comes forward and plays an Irish bagpipe alongside the band.

And then the chant. Everyone says it now.

'The Brets. The Brets. The BRETS OOT NOO!!!'

The carpenter tells me about the Khaki scouts. They are the Scottish Friends of the Irish Republican Army, on an anniversary jaunt to London. He introduces me to one, a man called Graham. 'Bloody Sunday,' Graham confirms. 'Good, isn't it?'

'Yes,' I nod, a trickle in my pores. 'Welcome to London.'

The march grows stronger. And the pipes. And the chant grows louder. The sublime back section merges itself with the boisterous front and all is similar. The families, once sedentary, are saying it. Standing and saying it and facing the stage. It can be heard down the entire High Street. I am sure of it. I think of the bobbys, oozing down the street like thick jam, and I hope they can hear it as well. Graham puts an arm around my shoulder and swivels me until I am staring squarely at the stage. I join in.

'The BRETS. THE BRETS. THE BRETS OOT NOO!'

Anita does not chant, but she does not stir, either. She smiles. And stares. Gemma nudges my shoulder.

'Claudia,' she says. 'I think we had better go.'

I shake my head. No chance.

My feet tickle with the marching rhythm. The music rips inside my ears and deep in my gut.

'THE BRETS. THE BRETS. THE BRETS OOT NOO!'

This is a perfect place for me, I ponder. I am young. I have nothing to surrender. I could give it up and go to Belfast. I will grow my hair out to its natural colour until it falls long and lank about my shoulders, allow my skin to fade to a startling winter white. I'll occupy a windowless room in Divis Flats. Throw stones at the British army from a fortress of council cement. Sell posters from an outpost of the Sinn Fein bookshop. Find a coal-eyed, muscular Provo with a set jaw and angry brow, and make love to him. Hide. Fight. Get the Loyalist bastards out of our land.

The chant perserveres, and so do my feet. I chant loudly, to be heard.

'THE BRITS. THE BRITS. THE BRITS OOT NOO!'

Of course, I will not go. I know this. But I love the feel of the magic march, that raw repeating thing that strikes beneath the bosom, rippling through my voice and body, strumming all my toes . . .!

'THE BRETS. THE BRETS. THE BRETS OOT NOO!'

Don't stop.

perry and isabelle

Ah, Perry and Isabelle. Feline. Tall. Skin like an elephant's tusk, and thick black hair pouring dogged and heavy on sharp, square jaws, stubborn mouths, those dark and even features. As children, Perry and Crilly neighboured in a row of dwellings near the mental hospital. Crilly took me to the old town once; it was a sooty place just north of the city, bordered by cakey cliffs and a greasy sliver of sea and a forlorn lighthouse jutting into the grey Irish sky, flashing blurry and red through the low clouds, omitting a lackadaisical moo only from time to time. I liked the town, for all its drab and muted calm; it seemed a safe place to be. The houses looked like shambling tents of black straw, their terraces devoured by the glutton of rot, their roofs low and sloped as though faintly hovering from some old and finished war.

Together, Perry and Crilly committed endearing and devilish acts; climbing to the ceiling of the asylum chapel to ring the chapel bell at precisely the wrong time, loitering upon the roof of the geriatric ward in pursuit of fat blue-winged pigeons, throwing craps in front of the Sinn Fein bookshop. At the age of sixteen, Perry shot to his full height of six foot three, and his face, formerly hard and squinty and square, became stern and still and beautiful. To look at now, he is a spark of unreal; his eyes a most violent green, his skin a shock of white beneath the moorish black of his hair, but to listen to him is to hear yet another city boy, a Dublin lad, sprung from a family of twelve, none of whom resemble him but speak exactly like him, even his sisters. In his teens, he learned to drink and swore an allegiance to the pint. He condemned Crilly for his hash, and once went so far as to yank a steaming thick spliff from Crilly's hand and toss it down the lighthouse cliff. Not two years later, he was dealing smack in Ballymun where he met Isabelle at an unlikely pub near a client's flat. He was instantly taken by the oozy Frenchness of her and the fact that she looked so much like himself. She was a student of some sort, I don't know of what. He sold her heroin and they fell in love. They flew to Bombay the following spring, encased a two-grand package of smack in six Tibetan Buddhas and shipped the load to England. On their return to the United Kingdom, Perry was searched and questioned at Heathrow. He was sent to prison on the Isle of Man. Isabelle stayed in London and found a job as a nightclub hostess in Soho, taking monthly trips to the Isle of Man and sneaking gear to him through credibly sealed packets of Twiglets. He stayed in prison for one year.

I meet Perry for the first time at the Starry Arms in Kentish Town. He wears a silvery trenchcoat falling to his knees. It speaks to me, his coat, of high cliffs and low pavement and black December skies. He is poker-faced and icy-eyed. I think he will not be friendly, until I gather the nerve to talk to him and ask him — in a friendly way — about prison.

'Did you get clean?' I ask. 'In the beginning?'

He says sure, he was clean all right, and the screws left him nothing but a shit-soiled bucket and two aspirin to sort himself out with. But he relented at the sight of Isabelle smiling and bearing gifts, his Continental dream. He says that he is clean now; Issy and him have been off the stuff for five whole days.

'But aren't you dealing?' I ask hopefully.

He has to make a living. I breathe a sigh of relief and pleasure.

Crilly sidles in beside me with two double shots of Jameson's.

Perry fixes his gaze onto Crilly's; I am hurt that he has forgotten me so soon. But then, he gestures to both of us, inviting us in.

'Youse comin'?'

We go in my car. Perry directs me down to Euston Road and forgets to mention the turnoff, causing me to make a rather dangerous and illegal U-turn at King's Cross. I don't mind. Eventually, we reach the council estate, which is shaped like a square C and ominous in the absence of lighting (the bulbs having burnt themselves out of lamp-posts scrawny like something starved). Perry leads us up the unlit stairwell, the smell of urine sharp in our nostrils. On the rail of the terrace overlooking the car park sits a small tinker boy, his ginger hair matted with dirt, and his face plump and spotted by soot or chocolate. He concentrates on a derelict American car beneath him, which is without wheels and a windshield. He holds a soggy triangle of chips, the grease seeping through the paper. Though he cannot be more than five or six, he wears a man's anorak, badly zipped and uneven, a heap of purple fabric tilted to one side and a small freckled shoulder bare on the other. He turns to face us and smiles when he sees Perry. I am touched by his childlike affection and I half expect him to call Perry 'Uncle'.

'Oy, Romeo Bullocks,' he shouts, 'ye seen Shane tonight? Ye goin' op te' Heroes' Arms?'

'No, Christy,' says Perry, 'and why ain't ye got to bed? Where's your auld dear?'

'Fock knows. She's op te' Heroes, I 'tink. And 'tey won't be letting me in tonight.'

'Too bloody right,' says Perry, 'te' likes of yourself will lift everything tat ain't nailed down. You're only a baby, besydes.'

'I'm fockin' not. Ye' tink you're sometin' bot you're only tall. I seen Shane tonight. He's squatting te' flat at ground floor. His mum's moved te' cat in and a snake into te' bathtob!' The boy grins wildly. His eyes are huge.

'Is tha' right, Christy?'

'Aye. And te' ting is, when Shane takes his bath, he don't botter to move the snake out of te' tob!'

We share a hearty laugh, and ascend the final flight.

'He's a rogue, 'tat one,' says Perry. 'He comes in te' flat sometymes, nicks cigarettes from right under me nose.'

'He's cute, though,' I say.

'Aye. I suppose he's cute all right. Too fockin' cute, if you're askin' me.'

'No one's askin' you, Perry,' says Crilly in a jocular tone, 'and where's your fockin' keys?' Crilly's own accent broadens in the presence of Perry.

'Look at you, Crilly,' I say, nudging him, 'you're a real Jackeen. You'd better dig your Flann O'Brien out from behind the radiator.'

'Shut op,' says Crilly. 'What the fock do you know, Yankee pigdog. Ye tink you're some major aut'ority on te Irish race?' He turns to Perry. 'She thinks she's a radical 'cause she's been to West Belfast *once* and scribbled Bernadette Devlin's name in pencil on the Falls Wall!'

Perry opens the door. 'Well, it's more than most of 'tem ever fockin' do. And tha's includin' our own.'

'Not at all!' Crilly grabs my waist roughly and pulls me towards him. 'She's a pretty face is all,' he teases.

'Aye, I wouldn't argue wi' tha.'

I am in a good mood now. Crilly leads me into Perry's flat and seats me beside him on the orange settee. The sitting-room is small and close with an electric heater that has been left on.

'Isn't that dangerous?' I ask Perry, staring at the hot orange coil in its metal box.

'Aye, I'm always meanin' te shut it off when I go out, but I keep forgettin'.'

'You're gonna burn yourself out one of these days, Perry,' says Crilly.

Perry sits down and unravels six tiny envelopes, cut of magazine paper, on the low coffee table. 'It wouldn't be te' first toyme,' he tells us.

I watch his hands. He pours five envelopes onto one flattened paper square, and hands the sixth to Crilly.

'You got any foil, Perry?' asks Crilly. Perry motions to his right. Crilly makes for the kitchen. 'And will you bring me works as well?' Perry calls, 'and put te' water on!' Crilly returns three minutes later with a roll of aluminium foil, a spoon, a syringe, a box of kitchen matches and a mug of boiling water. 'I couldn't find the Vitamin C,' he declares.

'I've got it in me pocket.' Perry produces a small bottle of vitamin C from his trenchcoat. He prepares the works, while Crilly arranges the foil for us. Again I think of Christmas: the wrapping of gifts, of Larry's parents' house on Christmas Eve, presents strewn like polished stones, tinsel draping the tree like angel hair pasta, the fabulous grand piano and the window looking out on Fifth Avenue, Ella crooning from a discreet speaker in a cosy nook. I watch Perry's eyes narrow as he handles the needle, his coat still on. He does not so much sit as squat upon the rug, kneeled over the low table as though in prayer. 'See them boys at te' Rose and Crown?' he asks Crilly, 'tha fockin' Pete O'Callaghan. Gobshite 'tinks he's a rock star cause he's roadie for Paul's band. Keeps nattering about some demo he decydes is gonna make it for him. Yeah, he's a rock star sure enough, wit' his guitar in hock, his ugly mug juttin' out every which way. He's a promising specimen of a star till they find the needle up his elbow. And he tinks he ain't usin'! Always goin' on he don't have a fockin' "real" problem!'

'He told me he was going into treatment. In Dorset or somewhere,' says Crilly.

'Aye, he's always sayin' tha'. Last week it was Norwich.' Perry taps his needle for air bubbles. He begins to sing, in a distracted and toneless voice:

. . . as I was goin' over, te' Cork and Kerry mountains . . .

A key turns in the lock. An elegant and weary young woman appears at the door, dressed in a short maroon cocktail dress, her eyes slightly smudged by old pencil, her hair loose about her shoulders. Perry introduces me to Isabelle. She regards me with suspicion, but when I hold out my hand, she takes it. She greets Crilly coolly and takes her place on the floor beside Perry. Real twins, I think. And both wearing their coats in the stifling smelly heat of paraffin. I think she will kiss him, but instead she pushes up her sleeve. 'I'm exhausted,' she says in a low voice, her accent seriously French. 'Will you let me?'

Perry stares at her for a moment, and then examines her arm. 'You're bruised as anyting. Give me your hand.'

I am so intrigued I forget about Crilly, who is ready for me with an unwrinkled surface of silver, the smack neatly concentrated into a lump. 'C'mon Jez,' he says patiently, 'melt it down.' I take the tube and have my first puff and lean back upon the settee, my eyes closed, my legs spread slightly. Crilly follows me back and kisses me, drawing the residue smoke from my mouth. 'Do you want me?' I ask him after he has kissed me, his face hot and close.

'I want you something immense,' he says, 'and I love it like this, when we both feel the precise same way.' He pulls back and lights his own. I sit up and examine the room. There is a tiny black and white television on an orange crate. The walls are painted an avocado green and they are uncovered, but for a caricature sketch of Isabelle above the television set. There is one narrow window, sticking shut from the inside with paint and nails. A chair of grey-flecked green, fabric missing from both arms exposing splintery wooden posts, remains unsat in. The coffee table is a vinyl-surfaced thing bordered by a formica frame of yellow and lime flower designs; it reminds me of Tupperware. The ceiling is low and a mustard colour, though dry rot has seeped through and chipped most of it away, leaving whitish, gaping blisters. A faint smell of cabbage wafts from the flat next door. An underfed black cat settles, unnoticed, at Isabelle's side. I look back to the works. I have never seen them before, so close. Except in films. Perry and Isabelle are arguing.

'You know that you cannot do my hand,' says Isabelle, 'they will see it at work. Do my left arm.'

'I'm gettin' tired of this, Isabelle. I'll do your arm, but don't be complainin' if it fockin' well hurts. You're lookin' more like a battered wife every day.'

'This is a lie.'

She is right, she doesn't, though when I catch a glimpse of her left arm, her bruises are pink and prominent, crawling the length of it like squashed insects. Perry taps the needle one last time, taps her arm for veins and injects the syringe into a bruise. Isabelle grimaces. I can look no longer; I bury my face in Crilly's shoulder. I have never liked shots. As a child, I had to be held down to get my flu vaccination. Crilly laughs and puts his arm around me. 'You don't have to look at them,' he says, consoling me.

But I look again, in time to see the needle fill with Isabelle's blood. Isabelle leans back, takes her coat off, smiles and shuts her eyes. When she opens them she smiles at me.

'Crilly's told us so much about you,' she says. 'It's nice that you came around tonight. I understand you're at art school.'

'That's right,' I say. 'Are you interested in art?'

'I am more into film. In Paris I was very involved with a production company of Sabinet. They are sort of an avant-garde organisation of documentary and film verité.'

'What did you do?'

'A bit of everything, really. Acting, cinematography, you know, whatever was around.'

'Isabelle, if you won't do me I'm doing meself.' Perry is sulking, thrusting the needle in her face. Isabelle shrugs amiably as though to say 'boys will be boys,' and shoots Perry up easily in the top of his hand. Crilly hands me the tube. I take another puff, give Crilly a blowback, gaze happily about the room. 'I'm glad we did this,' I say to Crilly. 'I'm really enjoying myself. And they are so beautiful, and so much alike.' Crilly snuggles close to me. We gaze at the other couple as though we were watching cinema. Perry has taken a generous hit from his lover and is now nodding off. Isabelle nudges him and his head falls forward over the coffee table, tips of his hair brushing against the largest lump of heroin. 'Arrête, idiot!' Isabelle hits him and he jerks up his head, his eyes wide and glassy. The lump is more or less intact, though crumbs of it stick to Perry's fringe. We are all relieved. 'He always does this,' says Isabelle, by way of apology. 'Nobody's perfect,' I say. Isabelle watches as Crilly takes a burn, and lights another one for me. 'You are wise,' she says, 'to do it that way. It is very disciplined of you.'

'It isn't noble or anything,' I say. 'I'm just afraid of needles.'

'You are lucky,' Isabelle says. 'I am in love with the needle. But today, I don't have a very bad problem. Perry and me have been without it for five days before this only on methadone. Tomorrow, I will not be sick. It is so nice, like this, to finally socialise with you.'

Perry has fallen asleep, his long body stretched across the rug and floorboards. Isabelle throws him a maternal gaze.

'Are you going to France again?' I ask.

'Yes, I am going to Provence in the summer. It will be good for me.' Isabelle's lids grow heavy and she falls over, her head cocked to one side. Crilly is also nodding, but at the tinny thud of Isabelle's needle striking the floor, his eyes grow big as though he has lost something. He kisses me suddenly and hard. 'Let's go,' he says.

'Have you got the envelope?' I ask, feeling adult at last, the responsible wife.

'What's left of it.'

'Will there be any for tomorrow.'

'A little. Come, Jez.'

At the door I turn and look at Isabelle, who is half sitting up but asleep, her maroon dress neatly buttoned, her hair shiny and unmussed, her lips relaxed and full, her head heavy and turned to one side, her eyes glazed slits of half-slumber. 'She's so glamorous,' I say to Crilly.

'God love her. She doesn't like me,' he whispers.

'Why not?'

'She says I'm common.'

We put on our coats and shuffle out the door, leaving Perry and Isabelle warm and asleep in the glare of the paraffin heater.

the back room

Larry, my stepfather, was tired of off-Broadway plays in creaky old theatres that nobody ever came to see. He was wary of deodorant adverts. He wanted a career. He landed a part in a high drama cop show called *Bobby, the Assassin and Me*, and we moved to Los Angeles. They bought a Spanish villa rooted into the hillside at many levels, a house rumoured to have been built for Rudolph Valentino. Mom gave birth to a baby boy, and called him Winchell (not after the doughnuts, though the association would later cause him grief at school). Mother cut her hair short, wore high Italian heels as always, and co-produced a television film. Larry knocked down the partition wall between the dining-room and the kitchen. He got a small part in a hospital drama. Mom's film won an Emmy. Larry's hospital drama was off the air in six weeks. Mom produced another film. Larry lifted the sticky brown carpet, sanded down the hard wood floors, stripped paint from the high beams in the living-room. He got a new series. It failed. He opened a French restaurant in the Westside. It showed promise.

Daddy feared I would not be properly looked after. He thought my mother was a shrewd and bloodless Hollywood mogul. He told his friends. He wrote her a letter. He moved to Los Angeles to be near me. Soon, he was co-producing a soap opera with my mother called *Chicago Suite*. The soap was wildly successful. Larry did guest shots on it occasionally, but mostly, he cooked. Daddy bought a house in the Hollywood Hills, not half a mile from my mother's. It was a stark and modern slab overlooking the city, sporting a salubrious entrance with a brass-topped stairwell. He married his accountant's daughter in a hotel room in Las Vegas. They bore a child and then another. Carol was a short, tight-shouldered, emaciated woman with a high peroxide wedge of hair. She wore a blusher with flecks in it, and blue eye shadow. Her voice was a sharp, high squeak. She had a Long Island accent, though she came from Fresno. She quit her job as manager of the Automoto Insurance Company. As her second child grew within her, she convinced my father to branch out on his own, leaving my mother behind. His second, 'solo' soap, a Southern Dixie drama called *Salamander City*, received an outstanding citizen award from the President of the United States. Carol was proud. She decorated the house with great big marbled leapfrogs, two matching ones at the door.

In my father's house, I took the back room. It was not so much small as rectangular, with a low ceiling, two narrow windows and a slab of aquamarine industrial carpet, firm to the touch. Through the front window lay a sprawl of hills, but the window above my bed butted the neighbour's garage. The neighbour, a fifty-ish Iranian stockbroker, designed a mock-Disneyland moat on either side of his house, with spiralled gates and towers of purple and yellow, like a miniature golf course. I slept facing north. Upon awakening, I was stirred by the muted chug and hum of the neighbour's Cadillac.

The thing that struck me most about the room was its symmetry. A set of steel shelves backed the north wall, upon which propped a full desk unit: a tidy slab of bulletin board, an empty roll top desk with a formica surface, and a pencil sharpener. On the opposite wall, a print was mounted; an austere graphic design, white and grey to match. The room was painted in a cool shade of dusty grey; Wedgwood grey, a hint of blue, a matching bedspread upon the bed. I do not remember how or where this decor was chosen. Upon recollection, it seems to have been there when the house was bought, though I know it isn't so. I liked it once; it had the clean, easy authority of my father's office, and I felt it was a place in which hard work could be done. I would write a story on my new Smith-Corona; I would draw a host of painted women with my new 'complete' collection of Pentel pens. I was twelve.

I did none of these things. I dug my father's old short stories out from beneath the roll top desk and read them. They were unpublished stories, filled with the plight of his affairs: an art student, bundled in the winter snow and as bright as Easter, a girl, really. She was called Mandy and she met us, once, at the Metropolitan Museum of Art, bearing books for him, candy canes for me. He wept over her in Central Park; he said to me, when I was nine, 'My heart is broken'. Our sadness was immense. We spent the rest of the week at the cinema, stuffing ourselves hotly with popcorn so oily it stained our clothes. I remember Mandy well; her tapered nails, the fragrant neck, that just-in-out-of-the-cold feel to her fingers, the festive bob of her hair. She reminded me of my mother when I (or she) was very young; the perfume upon my mother's neck when she leaned over to say goodnight, a pearl of jade clinking warmly and lightly upon my chest, Mommy on her way to the Village Gate, to meet some dark Europeans, to catch an excellent set of jazz. I read the story many times. There was another woman called Helen. She dropped cans of root beer all over my feet in the subway station; one broke and splattered and dampened my toes. The affair did not last long, but he got a short story out of it. 'It's worth it,' he said to me once, 'if you can write about it.' Sometimes I asked about these stories. He shrugged them off as he would soft core porno. He said they were the self-indulgent ramblings of a patches-on-the-elbow peasant, and who the hell did he think he was anyway? Now, he wore expensive grey suits, relinquished all pipe smoking, and drove a BMW. He still liked Irish music; I liked his liking, the exuberance of banjos duelling through the hollow bedroom walls when he was home.

I read *Seventeen* magazine. I ate chocolate Zingers snuck into my school bag after school. I did not throw the papers away. They accumulated beneath the television until they threatened to be seen, at which point I smuggled them out of the house in my knapsack. I don't know why I kept them for as long as I did. I lived in fear of their discovery, and yet I kept them. If someone had wished to find them, they could have. But no one did, or at least, nothing was said.

Each morning, I made a list, in coloured pens, of the things I would do that day.

1. Begin diet.
2. Go to school.
3. Come home from school — do all of homework.
4. Write a short story.
5. Eat dinner.
6. Draw.

But . . . there were tacos and pound cake from the school catering truck, a eucalyptus tree in the park at recess to nap beneath, reruns of old sitcoms to watch in the evening.

One day I would sing torch songs in Rio, write five best-sellers in London, have no children, or live in a brownstone in New York, all by myself. Life was a grid of stucco through which the clichés were sought. I lived for the clichés, I awaited them. Homework was irrelevant. I couldn't do it, couldn't bring myself to turn the pages of my notebook. Too many pages had already been unturned — it was too late now.

Marcus, a senior with a smooth black face, drove me home from school. He was always late starting. He loitered in the parking lot, pleasantly bemused by the coquettish chatter of juniors who courted him. He drove his car (a BMW, used) in a quick, staccato rhythm in time to an 8-track cassette of the Doobie Brothers.

Carol did not let me have a key of my own.

In contrast to the prairie-like flatness of the structure, a grand gold and white awning prefaced the house. I climbed the high stairs breathlessly as though there were many more of them than there were.

The bell was loud and clear as a chime. I rang, sucked in my stomach, adjusted my knapsack (already tattered and heavy with the weight of unread textbooks, crushed pound cake and dull-pointed pencils). I listened for footsteps. I forced rhetoric into my head: be nice and friendly, volunteer information about school, ask if you can help in the kitchen. In that order. She answered. Her hair was stiff and phosphorous, a dome-like wedge. Her eyes were heavy beneath streaked green lids.

I spoke. 'Hi.'

She said it too. She said it barely. Hi.

Her sound was but a squeak, a mumble. She retreated into the kitchen. Resisting the temptation to take refuge in my room, I deposited my knapsack and followed her, holding my breath, staring straight ahead.

'Did you have a good day?' The kitchen was a foreign place, and always; centred by a cutting board, formica shelves the colour of butter and wicker, low ceilings and no windows. I stood at the doorway, waiting.

'It was all right.' Carol busied herself with dishes and paper bags. There were always groceries, and her baby lay sleeping beside her in a cushioned basket, wicker like the shelves.

'What did you do?'

'Oh, nothing special.'

'Such as?'

'You know what I do.'

I didn't really.

'Well, did you buy a birthday present for Grandma?'

'Yes, I did that yesterday.' Her words were brisk, like the beak of a bird, and nasal.

'Can I watch a video?'

'Wait until your dad comes home.'

Stand up straight, I said in my head. Improve your posture. Ask her why.

'Can't I watch one now?'

'I would rather you waited.' Her eyes averted, downcast.

'Why?'

But I knew why. I was not allowed in the master bedroom without supervision. This was one of Carol's rules. I was also forbidden to answer the kitchen phone before she did. I knew that she was operating on a matter of some principle, something basic and territorial, something she had been taught, perhaps. I pursued it anyway. I waited to see her face tense as if it was an airtight balloon on a stick; never mind that it made me choke somewhere in my chest. It gave me the impression of having worked for something and, once defeated, I could take my comfort in the cool blandness of the back room. At least I had tried.

I wanted to say, I know there are no genuine secrets in that room. Your room. Your master bedroom.

The room, the master bedroom, was a dark, meticulous chamber of matching pillowcases and flesh-toned carpet, floral prints on the wall and a bedspread to match, identical bedside tables without drawers, a wardrobe of tall discretion, a VCR. My own mother's bedroom was a bright white gallery fronted by an old Mexican balcony overflowing with fuchsia and courting pink wildflowers. An oil painting of shocking reds, bought from an obscure Peruvian painter, cried out from above the bed. The bed occupied a high platform of stained pine. There were mirrors and a bovine settee of turquoise and, adjacent to this, an array of handmade metal shelves, varying in size, sloppy and cosy with books, and an antique radio-lamp to glisten yellow and red in the evenings only. A 'Poor Pitiful Pearl' doll, once belonging to a great-aunt, draped from a high shelf. And there were more books. And a cassette deck crooning the blues and Bach. Only that. My mother's room was teeming with secrets. I wanted to tell Carol. Real secrets, they were: the knotted bag of marijuana and zig-zags in Larry's rickety old night table, a forgotten wad of Italian cash at the bottom of a dusty cat-jar, the dildo in the underwear drawer, several adult videos. (I watched the videos once, because they were rated X, but I found them terribly dull, and the leading man looked like my girlfriend's father. I told my mother, and she agreed.) I was always allowed into my mother's room, despite the secrets. Or nearly always.

Once, in a rare burst of temper, Carol said, 'Your mother didn't want you, she tried to abort you. And why wouldn't she?' I retorted, she isn't Catholic.

Carol's kitchen was silent but for the hum of the refrigerator. Why did she never listen to music? Didn't she hear it, the drone, the hum, that awful, teasing, dreary hum? I didn't dare to ask. My stomach knotted and queasy, I posed but one last question.

'When is my father coming home?'

At around seven. Always at around seven. Dragging myself down the unlit hallway floor like a slug, I coiled myself back, back to the back room, and ate and waited.

Though the back room was officially 'my room', I began to hate it. I spent hours there, evenings, days, late nights. Years. Listening to AM radio. Trying to memorise the top ten. Reading *Seventeen* from cover to cover; making lists of the fall fashions and vowing to buy them when I was thinner, older.

Sometimes I phoned my mother.

'Could I come home tomorrow?' I would ask.

'I thought you were staying till Friday.'

'Maybe I could go home tomorrow and come back on Sunday.'

'Well, ask your father. What's she like today? Is it awful? What's she wearing?'

'Oh, the same. Mommy?'

'Yes, honey.'

'Can we have a dinner party for my birthday? With all your friends?'

We could. She would ask Joe and Mary and Stanley and Clarice. And she would bake a chocolate mousse torte.

I stalled, saying, 'Mommy, I want to go home.' She said she knew; 'Baby, I know.'

There were sounds in the background. Infant Winchell babbling. The sizzling of Larry's huge kitchen grill. Larry talking to a friend. Cutting up arugula. Mom had to go. I hung up the phone and wondered who else to call. Sometimes I called her back. Sometimes I held onto the receiver without putting it back into its cradle; distractedly, I held it, with Kool and the Gang wafting from the radio. When the radio began to grate, I turned it off and spread myself out on the bed, using the knapsack as a pillow, and then when it got too sharp, making dents in the back of my head, I took it away and lay flat. I failed to turn on the light when the sky grew dark and heavy. Twilight threatened to swallow my sight; I did not dare to defy it. At dusk, there was only the news. I sat and listened, to the radio which was not turned on, to the television whose volume was mute, naught. I sat and tried to hear, waiting for the sound of my father's key in the lock, when I could emerge from the back, into the front, maybe, the dining-room. But now, as evening dust blackened the room, and my loose black hair pressed dead against the sheet, I lifted my hand and looked at it. There was nothing else to do. I watched my fingers fade before my face.

pamela watkins

They say that Pamela Watkins is an English rose in denial. Any attempt she makes to obscure her femininity backfires with absurd vengeance; there is no refuge for that face of hers. Though I am envious, I would never think of competing. I accept that whatever good looks I may possess are artful, concocted at large by paint and persona. In truth, I suspect that I am bland. At times I enjoy my plainness; it is young and puerile to me in the bathroom mirror, the mirror that steams from my bath. I do not feel competitive with Pamela as I do with other women, because Pam, in her unwitting splendour, is not pretty as other women are. She is not coquettish, nor is she glossy or pristine. I have seen old pictures of Pamela; I have seen her pretty. I have seen her in hats, in high boots, in fishnets, in stilettos. I have seen snapshots of her arms extending cigarette lighters, her lips painted seamlessly in China red matt, each eyebrow plucked and lined with one rich stroke of a black pencil, false lashes on her eyes, 'twinkle' blue kohl beneath and drawn at a tilt. I've seen her looking Greek, Egyptian, Japanese.

Now she wears nothing but the same thing, and always. Her trousers have no heritage that anyone can define. Her boyfriend found them in the back of his van, abandoned by someone months or years before their discovery, and they have collected chocolate stains from half-eaten Minstrels and white smears from Quaker oats. They carry with them a distinct smell of metal, tar and petrol. Pamela washed them once and will not bother to wash them again until they are saturated with her own smell, not a bad smell, made up as it is of tea, musk oil, turpentine and taramasalata. Pamela is a sculptor, the sort that wittles her nights away until interest is shown in her work, at which point she abruptly withdraws. Once it is forgotten again, she resumes her work in the spartan room allocated to her by a local co-op.

Through the years and a mess of assorted lovers, four changes in location and layers of silt (from art and carpentry) which cling to her pink and olive skin like something tropical, she has succeeded in relinquishing prettiness. She turns up at plays and concerts with her baggy man's trousers belted at precisely the wrong curve of her hip, and her hair loose and slightly oily. On her face she wears only a slash of red lipstick smattered across her mouth in brazen defiance of the rest. Breezing by on her bicycle which she rides all the time, she appears as a sort of escaped young refugee, from Poland or some Dickensian work camp.

But there is no concealing her. For all her industrious androgyny she is more beautiful than ever. I have seen Pamela standing amidst fair and nimble-limbed Continental women, raven-haired leggy nymphets ten years her junior, and those local platinum finger-waved blondes, well-primped and perfectly petite; and still, they are outdone. Whenever she attempts to dress herself, in the event of someone's wedding, she scours my wardrobe, giggling girlishly at herself, throwing off her garments as though she is a small child trying on school clothes for a mother or aunt. I help her.

I paint her face and do her hair. When she is finished and suitably stunning, regally stunning, I am disappointed. She lacks the bare surprise of her own real features: the solid cheekbones ruddy with tiny veins in the cold, the wideness of her mouth, the black slant of her eyes, the strong patrician nose. Shameless, is her face in its unaided solitude.

One evening Pamela comes alone to my flat and speaks of Nigel. They have had a row. She hit him and he held her head in the toilet bowl while eating tomatoes on toast. The irritating thing is, he could not be bothered to put the sandwich down during the whole scene, and when she surfaced, she found his lip dripping with tomato seeds. Disgusted, she went out and had sex with a sixteen-year-old boy in the unlocked bathroom of a neighbourhood squat party. Nigel was annoyed, but he also found it funny. They borrowed a car and drove to Cornwall, though between the two of them they were virtually penniless and had to make do with beans on brown bread for the entire weekend. Their borrowed car collapsed in an anguished brown heap by the coast. It is still there. The owner, a Texan woman called Joyce, is far too besotted with both Nigel and Pamela to possibly object, and seems lackadaisical about retrieving it.

It is only ten o'clock. The pubs have closed; our friends will not yet be at Paprika's Café. We stop for passion cake and fried bananas. Paprika's is a tiny restaurant whose walls are covered in extinct record covers (Julie London, Vicky Carr), menus which have nothing to do with its own, candid photographs of mouths and patrons eating. We sit against the wall, beneath a slogan reading 'Rescue My Foot' which has been spray-painted not by a patron, but by the owner, Abel. Abel is a fortyish man with round unblinking eyes and a perfectly circular head. He manages several local bands and runs a private record label called 'How Many Buses'. One of his bands are at the Paprika tonight; they are called Dance Lance and they consist of three limber, head-shaven, androgynous boys who all knight themselves with the same name, which is Ron. Ron One goes nowhere without his cat, Stepson, on a tartan lead. Ron wears a kilt, a pair of orange Day-Glo tights, heavy green military boots, a pink macramé tank top and a yellow trenchcoat. He carries a Star Wars lunch-box in which he keeps old tube tickets,

cigarettes, make-up and money. Abel plays with his overwhelming sound system; on bounces a heavily tampered cover
of 'Dancing Queen', cut intermittently with a Scottish rap. Ron
Two, who is more effeminate than Ron One though less wildly
dressed, stands on a table. He likes to sing along. 'You can sing!'
he shrieks, shaking his hips. 'You can dance! Having the time of
your life!'

We laugh. We love the Rons. 'Christ,' says Pamela, good-
naturedly, 'do you think we can have a few more poofs in here?'
Ron Two winks at Pam and continues to sing. Ron One sits
down beside us. He tells me he is soon to release a single on his
own. I am not to tell the other Rons. We finish our cake and
plantains, and start on the wine. When I have finished my meal,
I roll a joint. Stepson, a short-haired cat of some unaccountable
breed, jumps up beside me on the seat. The smell of hash is
strong. Abel comes running out from the kitchen. 'We have to
be careful,' he says, sitting down, reaching for the spliff.

'Here.' I put the joint in his mouth. He relaxes and tells me
about a new band he is producing.

Occasionally the police drop by to complain about the noise,
but they do so only after midnight, and they fail to notice the
incessant smell of dope, sharp as burning leaves. One time,
during a late lock-in at the Paprika, I ran to the car to get my
cigarettes, and saw my friends through the Christmassy frost of
the window: silhouettes dancing, milling about and smoking;
the cone-shaped joints, most unmistakable in their size, dancing
from hand to hand. A policeman walked by, wished me good
evening and ushered a warning. It was about the strobes.

'You want to watch those strobes luv,' he said, 'they'll give
you amnesia,' and walked on.

We leave the Paprika. It is not cold. Pamela suggests that we
walk down the Prince of Wales Road to the Aegean Sea.

The Prince of Wales Road is dim for stretches, lit solely by broken yellowed ovals falling deftly from tall street lamps onto scarred pavement. We pass the desolate grounds of a school, fenced in by barbed wire and patches of trodden grass. We pass a council estate and a forlorn shop which seems to have been carved into the ground level of the estate. An elderly Indian woman in a sari is closing up and bringing down the grated gate. The road grows bright at the Mother Shipton pub. From within, I catch the trill of a Pogues song. The song feels right, apropos to a midnight jaunt, a walk with a good friend. It stays inside of me . . .

> As I walked down by the riverside
> one evening in the spring
> Heard a long gone song from days gone by
> Blown in on the great North wind
> Though there is no lonesome corncrake's cry
> of sorrow and delight
> You can hear the cars
> and the shouts from bars
> and the laughter, and the fights
> May the ghosts that howled
> round the house at night
> never keep you from your sleep
> May they all sleep tight
> down in Hell tonight
> or wherever they may be . . .

We are craving wine and baklava. The Aegean Sea is a Greek restaurant which stays open till three a.m. The pubs have closed, and it is crowded. We find seats in the front section, at a table shared by four Irishmen, diligently engaged in an in-ebriated medley of Beatles songs, improvising their own lyrics. Six Middle-Eastern businessmen sit sternly to our left, over a bottle of retsina and three plates, messy and strewn with houmous and broken pitta. Behind the counter, the fat Greek chef stands in good stead, his apron cheerfully stained, a generous plate of souvlaki in hand. He is always there. When he sees us, he smiles in recognition. The restaurant clogs quickly into a cosy fire hazard. The clearing swarms with secretaries and punks, locals and junkies, chatting, sweating, awaiting a beer or a meal for the road, but in no real hurry. At our table, one of the Irishmen has fallen asleep, his head collapsed in a puddle of beer. A big-boned, red-haired Irish woman tears through the crowd, stands squarely in front of us despite pushing from all sides and glares down upon us, her gaze steady, her freckles flushed. She throws down an empty glass, just missing the head of the sleeping man. The glass does not break.

'You're not me fucking father, right!' she yells at the sleeping head. He does not stir. She yells it again. 'You're not me fucking father, right!' Nothing. She turns on her heels and tears through the crowd once more and out the door. The others gaze after her in a casual way and resume their Beatles medley.

'Claudia,' says Pamela. 'Why don't you sing for us?'

I take a sip of wine and begin to sing.

> Of all the stars that ever shun,
> not one does twinkle like your pale blue eyes . . .

They all know the words to this one. The sleeping man lifts his head and sings along with his friends.

> . . . No matter where I wander I am haunted by your name
> The portrait of your beauty stays the same
> sailing on the ocean wondering where you are
> if you'll return again
> where is the ring I gave to Nancy Spain . . .

Pamela laughs. 'You're a hero, Claudia,' she says. She's right. I know all the words.

When we emerge from the restaurant, it is late. We are tired. We catch a mini-cab and share it back to Kentish Town. We stop at my flat first.

'Do you want to come to a Finnish film festival at the ICA tomorrow?' asks Pamela.

'Sure,' I kiss her and run into the house, for by now the air has turned crisp and cold. I fall into bed without taking my make-up off. The 'Nancy Spain' ballad reels round in my head even in sleep. Soon, there is pounding on the window, the pounding of the Rons, Roger and Simone, Crilly and Pamela, who has had a second wind. I am almost too drunk to hear them. But not drunk enough.

My North London flat is filled with neon. I collect it from a dusty shop in Hackney run by tall Italian twins. I like the desert green for the cusp of the evening, Caribbean pink for the smallest dot of night, yellow, white and red for post-pub crowds. The ooze of blue and blues. The pulse of pink. The bass of red and reggae. What is this place? Pedestrians might ask one another. A cafe? A nightclub? A brothel?

No, it is my home.

Hash is abundant; I keep a steady supply of Moroccan in a Japanese basket on the mantelpiece. It is my social catalyst, a lump of oil by which to lubricate the scenario that is my home, clamorous, everchanging, unhumble. Without the brown lump, I feel inadequate as a hostess, abbreviated in my domestic duties, incomplete.

There are the quiet, maudlin times: injured parties, slighted lovers, Chet Baker playing to serenade them. There are nights of anarchy: friends of friends and rivals in my home, rowing couples, drunken hooligans who sometimes break the neon. I invite anarchy as a rebuttal to my greatest fear: the fear of isolation or even worse, the fear of mediocrity. I do no productive work; I never really go to art school.

I sing in a band, from time to time, a woman's band, sort of a makeshift bossa nova affair, though not one of us can play a thing and we always need help from the boys. We have a laugh.

I take stock of my bodies, my friends. I am holding court, lady of the mansion. You can sit where you like as long as it isn't in this chair, this armchair, my armchair, the one with the dancing balls splattered loudly across its back and arms, across its stained and silver gut. Live bodies are strewn restlessly about the flat, hands and eyes in ashtrays and record discs, tangerines and Rizlas, magazines and carpet and kebab wrappers, delving into the laps of one another, sparring opinions like rubber balls, reconciling in smoke and stereo and wide, generous laughing things.

I first meet Crilly on a crowded Thursday night in my local pub. We smoke a joint in my car. He is smartly dressed, deeply-voiced, handsome. He talks to me about Ireland, about the troubles. He is angry and dark, but courteous, with a heavy concerned brow, hot and engulfing hands, a paternal smell of brandy about him, a stern and steady timbre to his voice. He is aggressive and kind.

Friends warn me about Crilly. They admit he is charming, but fingers point to his eyes as warning signs, demonic pin points.

I tell him if he harbours any ideas about staying with me, he'd better kick the gear. He doesn't argue. He agrees.

But before he does, I add as an appendix, 'Won't you give me a taste?' He averts his eyes at my request. He refuses, as any gentleman would. Later, when I ask again, he is silent and I can feel him relent. I ask again. He gazes about the living-room, and he says it belongs to too many. He is tired of competing with my friends and their heavy leather jackets, cramped into my floor and furniture, and those clankish guitars, owners unknown, propped unsteady against the table. Bits of spliff, a comb that is not mine, Bukowski books belonging to no one, stuffed up in a pile beneath the telephone. This is one thing we can share in solitude.

Give us a taste, just once, and then we'll live like monks

forever, in a tapered bed and a kitchen that smells of Pine Sol.
Give us a taste.

On our next date, he has gear. Feigning fatigue, we urge a baffled
party to evacuate before the witching hour. Crilly sets me up
with a tube and foil. He runs the match beneath while I hold the
tube in my mouth, in the light of the desert green neon, with
Billie Holiday oozing from the stereo.

'Just follow the smoke,' he instructs, 'and hold it in. Keep
holding in no matter what.'

There is a syrupy peace in the hollow of my chest. Everything
is filled. I have never been so happy. I go into the bathroom,
vomit easily, and return. I am elated. And Billie singing her
blessed heart out like she never has before. And my wonderful
blessed friends home and safe in their respective blessed beds.
And the handsomest Celt on earth kneels before me while I sit
snugly in the big armchair, the best armchair. Again. And again.

Crilly, I have never known a man like you. Tell me more. Tell
me about Bobby Sands and your mother. Do it and do it more.

Claudia, oh Claudia, you are so beautiful. My mother was
gruff but she loved us. My sisters dressed me up in their dresses
and paraded me down the road and we listened to Van and I
learned to love Van. You are so beautiful. I am so lucky. It is like
you're not even real.

I'll tell you, Crilly, about my first trip to Scotland and the men
in chip shops who call you 'Hen' and the lads wearing green
Celtic scarves at lunchtime and broad pointy-horned cattle and
graveyards macabre with the tilting of tombstones caked with
moss and weeds, sheep grazing and weaving amongst them, and a
coastal fishing town in Harris where a night sky shimmers only
to itself and I am without friends from the real world and I listen
only for the sound of the tin whistle while the boats rock gently
in the jetty and the sky rages from beige to black and craggy

mountains dart until forever and a fisherman stands, stunning and alone, strong and unnamed, and leads me slowly into that everchanging sea.

I'll tell you about Penny Lane, my tiniest youth, I was tiny, so tiny, too tiny to spit on, and my friend Chock who lived in the bathroom radiator, hissing low inside my head, shrivelling at the clink of my mother's heels in the hallway, holding his breath, whispering, a lady is coming, dancing to the plaid of the bathroom tiles and to the records my father played; and the first time we heard 'Penny Lane', we knew we had heard it before.

There was a tapered garden on a hill, before those houses in a row, and though I did not understand reincarnation, I knew, he told me, about a narrow road smelling sweetly of petrol and roast potatoes, and though I'd never been, Chock had been, it was only across the street but I couldn't see it, he could see it, he told me so, and pointed to the ornate roof across the street, at the chimneys springing from a platform like stalks of green marble, the roof framed by edges intricately ribbed like steeples or the currents of the sea.

A pretty nest is selling puppies, he said, and sang to me of a nest (not nurse) from which puppies are hatched and sold, and there was a fireman and pedestrians with raincoats and walking-sticks, strolling the length of the roof as though it were an avenue, with a bright barber shop perched upon an antenna whose rust I couldn't see. I did not know England. I did not know Liverpool. I knew Penny Lane and it was, alas, enough Crilly, and when my father came one day and asked what I was looking at, I said Penny Lane and he stood for awhile and looked for awhile, while the roof held its breath it seemed and then he said, after all that standing and all that looking, he said, 'You're right', and hoisted me up upon his shoulders.

I'll tell you about Ryan Buck, fifteen years my senior, an ex-felon, an actor, my first, though my mouth was raw with the metallic taste of braces fresh on my teeth, and my features were like crooked, accidental things. He wore a red bandana and drank white Russians and quoted Kerouac and spoke loudly in superlatives and sang along to the radio in a shrill and grating soprano. His body was rich with the smell of sweat and kahlua and he sent me sprawling and hyper with untold hormones upon the bathroom tiles, but one day, suddenly, actually it was night, parked atop Mulholland Drive with the car windows steamed and the upright stick shift pressing painfully against my lower back and my head banging against the passenger door, I was paralysed by the heaving horny heaviness of him and my climax was full and first — first time ever — but followed by a limpness in my body, dull as the shade of putrid beige, and later I dreamed he had invaded me in sleep and crushed me with his broadness and with pillows, though Crilly it was not suffocation I feared, no, it was something more abstract, more bodily and carnivorous, something akin to nameless reptiles, and it was not so very different from the gun and the windbreaker blowing large and puffy about a stranger's gut like a tent in my car at Pico Boulevard, and I so sure I would be found dismembered and crotchless and gory and absurd, strewn from limb to limb across the green tweed upholstery, unrecognisable in death, and again the windows steamed, the windows steamed with that hot clenched nameless fist inside me and the glide of cool metal against my neck, and then there were no thoughts, no words in my head, nothing.

Crilly, I'll tell you about the sparkle of Belgravia, the shimmer of white marble, a sumptuous, salubrious white, the sugary white of fluffy friendship, cloudship, feely white, and the slim cobblestone road which led to the river where I met James who was fresh from Waterstone's with his arms full of Pinter plays, O he was as a young Terence Stamp, Crilly, but for the sly cracks of wisdom about the corners of his eyes, and we drank espresso and

he told me about Spain and the high mountains of India, and the
Pyrenees he had taken on foot, and though I was as trite as my
shopping Saturdays and my small muggy and squirming palms in
summertime, he painted my body swirly-lined and peach upon a
large canvas and made love to me upon the tip of the Heath
with all of London a basin of rooftops beneath us while the sky
loomed low in grey and pink, the Heath a dark pudding of
sloping mountains, wild and white and wide as Brontë country,
with only the smug suburban cliffs of Highgate Village peering
from behind its sprawling hem, and big dogs scurried like brown
birds to the crevice of foothills and then disappeared, so we
made love for a while beneath that sky, which cast a blaze upon
us the colour of cream.

I can't talk now I have gone so limp and languid and sugary with
my flesh stretched and itching, so Crilly carries me to bed. He
tends to me as one would a convalescent child delirious with a
terminal but ticklish illness; he tends to the outermost hazards
of my body (he is so violent and so tender) and back to a cave of
foetal musk, molested by warmth. The light of day will soon be
superfluous; and just as soon, it will frighten and appal me. I
don't care. I stay with Crilly. At last, I stay.

dublin

One damp evening late in autumn, Crilly receives word of his mother's train wreck. The train, en route to a religious pilgrimage in a place called Knock, was derailed by a solitary cow and tipped onto its side. Siobhan, Crilly's mother, bashed both of her legs in the accident, though this did not keep her from crawling to the aid of those more severely injured than she. She saved a friend's arm and a cousin's handbag. She is now in hospital in Dublin. I watch Crilly after he has heard the news from his sister, Megan. He sits on the bed for twenty minutes, sweating and smoking. Presently, he asks if I will go with him to Dublin. I say I will. The following day is spent in preparation; persuading my bank manager to extend my overdraft, procuring a letter of transference from Geraldine at the methadone clinic, gathering supplies for the journey. To contribute to our funds, Maggie gives Crilly two hundred tabs of acid to sell in Dublin. My car is clamped two hours before we are to leave for Holyhead, though lifted within the hour, after much persuasion and a torrid sobbing session at the clamping office. I return haggardly, as though I have been in a street fight, grotty from rushing and weeping and random taxicabs. The sun is setting. Crilly has procured six £20 bags and, in a burst of generosity, Perry donated a 200ml bottle of methadone to our cause. We smoke the first bag, throw a heap of indiscriminate clothing together and set off on our long journey to Wales, our bodies leaden and our lids heavy.

Still, I am excited. A journey. A motor trip. The sameness of yellow road lights, shaped like faucets, flash black flash upon the desert of the motorway, and then, the bit where the road goes dark, where there is no light at all, but for the torch-like eyes of our own headlights. I have made similar journeys many times, with Anita: left London at four a.m., arrived in Glasgow by midday. We sang songs and ate foam-tasting cinnamon pastries at gaudy roadstops, in places shaped like bugs with high modern bridges above the road. Granada. Rank. Trusthouse Forte.

This journey is a little different; boats and maps and the challenge of getting there. And I have never been to Ireland.

As Crilly cannot drive, I ply myself with junk food and coffee, preparing myself for the wheel. The car is shaky as a tractor, heaving with the warning groans of broken parts, the rev of an angry engine. The night is clear but very black. Crilly falls asleep, much to my irritation. Without his attention, I am martyred to the wheel. We reach the Welsh border in five hours, but soon lose our way and travel thirty miles in the wrong direction, during which we are stopped by the Welsh police. I shuffle through the glove compartment for my registration, MOT and insurance papers. The policeman is civil and he lets me go, commenting on my eyesore of a car, warning me to get my tail-light repaired.

I charmed him, I say afterwards. Crilly sleeps.

I know I'm on the right route when I spot a bus marked 'Pensioners Touring Kerry'. Crilly wakes and tells me about when he was little and slept in the same room as his father, while his sisters slept with his mother. He awoke one morning with his eyes glued shut from condensed cigarette smoke; his mother had to prise them open with solution. He tells me about the day his father died of liver failure; Crilly was only five. He was not permitted to attend the funeral, and three older neighbour children were appointed to look after him. But, through a

tawdry heap of bushes, he watched the procession and the bare
wooden coffin lifted by altar boys. He tells me of the only time
he has seen his mother drink; her infant grandchild vomited on
her coat, and she spouted a fine, volatile performance,
screaming Christ Almighty the cross a woman has to bear,
taking the Lord's name in vain for the very first time.

When sleep threatens to take him from me yet another time,
I remind Crilly of a line from the film *Drugstore Cowboy*, in
which the heroine says, 'You never fuck me and I always have to
drive'.

'But I do *fuck* you,' reminds Crilly. 'Frequently.'

I can't argue with this, but I urge him to include driving
lessons in his New Year's resolutions. I want to share the wheel
with him, to feel his power behind it. I want to be languid as he
steers, to navigate with my hands and eyes free.

We reach the port twenty minutes before the ferry is set to
sail. It is one-forty in the morning. In the muted streetlight,
Holyhead is almost picturesque, with whitewashed sandstone
cottages and the rippled shine of the moon upon the harbour.
We buy our tickets and drive onto the bottom level of the boat,
which reeks of fish and steel and human excrement. We ascend
the stairwell and buy drinks in the ferry lounge which is a wide,
low-ceilinged room lavish with yellow and orange. A huge
fluorescent butterfly-shaped tube of rotating yellow and orange
lights beams from an adjacent wall. We sit. Much to our
confusion, the entire boat crew is Polish and speak scarcely a
word of English. A muffled announcement is made over the
loudspeaker. The accent is too broad to understand. (It is later
explained to us that as Irish workers are on strike, a Polish crew
has been assembled.)

The boat sets off. We stuff our faces with scampi and chips.
(The scampi is dodgy; later I will throw up in the smelly boat
toilet.) An all-Polish ensemble, dressed in loud pantsuits of

yellow and orange and red, performs 'Girl from Ipanema' and other Latin favourites on an electric piano and Day-Glo drum set, before the electric butterfly. One old Irish couple slow-dances alone. They dance for hours. Or rather, they do not so much dance as cling to one another, rocking drunkenly with the tide. The woman has bleached orange hair and a shapeless tweed skirt; the man wears a rust-coloured suit and a bawdy fifties style tie, and a top hat. We are their only audience. We watch in silence. At one point, at some point, very late, the old man breaks away from his partner, and spins easily on a shiny patch of yellow floor, his long arms folded to his sides, not dancing at all now but simply spinning, spinning, for quite a while. It is four a.m.

'Look,' says Crilly, 'he's gone freelance.'

The Polish-Latin musak band continues to play. To our left, an Irish family of six eat salmon-paste sandwiches without speaking. We sleep.

We sail into Dun Laoghaire at seven a.m. The car queue is not long and I am excited by the welcoming signs in Gaelic. We drive to Swords and pick up a key from Crilly's sister, Lorraine, who occupies a small semi-detached house with her husband and her two children. Lorraine is tall and neatly-featured; her tone is dry and caustic. She gives us a cup of tea at the kitchen table. She says that Siobhan will not stop asking after her Marks and Spencer coat, which was abandoned in the wreck. I can barely keep my eyes open. I cry. We sit in the living-room for half an hour while members of the family drift by, sleepy-eyed, preparing for work and school. Lorraine's elder son puts a Guns 'n' Roses cassette upon the stereo. Crilly and I look at one another. We are so awfully tired.

Eventually, Lorraine tells us the way to Siobhan's new house. We thank her, get lost in Swords village and finally find it.

Crilly tells me that his mother has worked all her life to pay

for this house. It is small, smaller than my flat, and tidy, purpose
built, near the airport. It has a modest kitchen in the back, and a
sitting-room partitioned on either side by wood-panelled doors,
frosted windows at the top of each. The first thing I feel is cold;
it seeps into my skin, soaks my limbs. Crilly drags the electric
heater into the sitting-room. We huddle together on the brown
carpet, between the beige and brown walls. The sickness of
morning is already upon us, unaccustomed as we are to being up
so early. I suggest we have a burn. There is no silver foil, so Crilly
sets us up with an empty chocolate wrapping from his pocket.
We smoke a bit of skag, feel better and nod off on the tweedy
settee before the heater. We are not due to visit the hospital
until six. Siobhan's bedroom is empty but for the pink carpet, a
bed with a pink bedspread and a chest of drawers rattling
vacantly from some obscure, whining wind. A Sacred Heart of
pink and maroon stands serenely upon one wall, reflected in a
small square of mirror upon the other wall. The room is very
cold. We huddle beneath the covers, but to our dismay, the one
duvet is but a slim pink layer of fabric resembling a furniture
cover. I fetch another from the guest room. Crilly reaches for
me but stops himself; we are in his mother's bed after all. We fall
asleep instantly and do not wake until five-thirty when Crilly's
sister Megan phones, instructing us to meet her at the hospital.

Crilly and I have a generous burn before leaving the house. I
shower quickly, spend some time painting my eyes, and select an
attractive outfit to the best of my ability, given my makeshift
twist of clothing. I settle on a simple cotton dress, black, and a
pair of dangling earrings. I put my hair up, belt my waist with a
red suede sash from Los Angeles and pencil my lips a deep red.
When Crilly is impressed by my appearance, I am also satisfied. I
have not dressed myself up for some time. It is gratifying to find
that I can not only look good, but I can look respectable too.
Crilly wears a smart blue shirt with the buttons done to the neck

and a pair of Italian trousers stolen from a shop in Covent Garden. He shaves, washes his hair and borrows a modest silver stud for his ear. Sufficiently stoned but not unreasonably so, we stand before the bathroom mirror, marvelling at the crisp clean surfaces of ourselves and one another.

'We forget how good looking we are,' says Crilly, and though his remark is meant to lift us, it makes me sad.

Palled by the bleak, dusty nooks of outer Dublin (my mother told me once that eventually, in some parts, all cities look like Brooklyn, and I'm beginning to see her point), I expect the hospital to be yet a stranger place. But the shock of white corridors refreshes, as do the nurses and strangers milling about, both the sick and the visiting, a comforting sight after our lonely day of dreamless sleep. I strain to hear clips of conversation; I long to hear Dublin in their voices, to feel that I am really here. I hear it often enough at home, but there is something vital about the brogue within its native walls; it makes me feel there is no ethnicity, no affectation, no accident about it.

It's difficult finding Siobhan. I don't mind. I enjoy the clink of our heels on linoleum, the perplexity of lifts and maps. I gaze about myself as I go, glancing through open doorways into clean white wards where patients sit erect in their beds eating trays of stew and potatoes, watching television from swivel sets on the wall.

Crilly doesn't feel the same. His body stiffens as we reach the ward, St Patricia's, fifth floor.

Siobhan has her own room. The door is open. Crilly takes my hand and leads me in. At first I cannot see her for the heaps of people about her bedside, brandished with packaged sweets and magazines and flowers of white and purple. Siobhan is wide awake, sitting upright in her bed. She is a pretty old woman with pure white hair and clear blue eyes, and skin that crinkles only slightly about the mouth and corners of her eyes. She wears a pink robe. Her legs are covered. She complains cheerfully as we enter saying, 'Jaz I've never had so many people kissin' me in all me life, strangers and all, you'd tink I was in Italy or England or America, God forbid!' Crilly kisses her. I think better of it. Her eyes are wide and curious upon my face, as though she knows the very name of me even without introduction. Yet Crilly moves aside and introduces me. When I extend my hand to her, she looks to Crilly before taking it. I am suddenly nervous.

'Rory,' she says to an elderly man sitting to my right, 'give the girl a chair now, won't you!'

I protest, but Rory leaps from his seat and I am obliged to fill it. I sit and fidget like a child. Siobhan embarks upon an extensive list of introductions. Rory is her second cousin. Frankie McCauley, a broad-faced man, is the local butcher. John and Sarah Walsh are neighbours from the old neighbourhood. Stevie and Patsy Mulligan are the sons of a dear friend who has recently passed away. Father Moore is only a brief visitor; he has called in crisply to pay his respects, exchange a few words of banter with Patsy (also a brother-in-law of somebody), and to inform Siobhan that next year he will be personally heading a pilgrimage to Knock so as to ward off any unfortunate flukes of the road. He leaves shortly. Siobhan identifies me to everyone as Claudia Coe, Crilly's girlfriend from America. Crilly stiffens again by my side, asking after other women who have been in the crash; he knows them all. Siobhan offers a story for each, and though the stories vary, her tone stays the same.

'Ah, Bernadette Kennedy. Her body's intact but her mind's amok, though if you're askin' me, I'd say that was nothin' new.

'Sally Dee Kavanaugh. Lost her arm but not her life, well lucky I'd say, given her position when the cattle hit.

'Ah, Theresa McCresh. That one wasn't so lucky.'

Crilly congratulates his mother on the purchase of her new

house. The older men in the room are fascinated by Crilly. They have not seen him since he was a boy.

'I see you've taken to wearin' that jewellery in your ear,' says Rory. Siobhan scoffs. 'Ah Jaz, he's has that 'ting done for ages!'

'Are you workin' these days, Crilly?'

Crilly shakes his head. 'I take what comes along.'

'By the look of your hands now I gather what comes along is good and scarce for you. Did you see the hands of your boy, Siobhan? Woman's hands, I tell you!' Rory laughs heartily.

Siobhan smiles to be polite.

'Well, Cousin Rory,' Crilly retorts, 'some of us here use other means to work with besides our hands!' Siobhan gives a good laugh this time. Her laugh is the same as Crilly's.

'O and Jasus, he's pickin' up a bit of that fancy Brit language!' pipes Patsy, motioning to me. 'You must have trained him well!'

'But I'm American.'

'Ah yes, America. What part of America are you from?'

'California.'

'I have a cousin there. In Orange County, I believe. Joey McNamara?'

'I don't know him.'

''Tank God for that. He's a miserly character, that one.'

A slim, smartly dressed woman appears at the doorway. She looks very much like Crilly, though her hair is cut and tinted like a soap opera actress. She is smooth-skinned and pretty, with a small nose, even lips, large green eyes, much mascara. Siobhan introduces her to me as Kimberly, her eldest daughter. Kim shakes my hand and tucks her briefcase behind the door. Her accent is gentler than the others, and her words are clipped as though she was schooled in England as child, though I know she wasn't.

'How are you getting on, Mum?' she asks.

'Ah I'm not too bad. They've got me doin' lift-up 'tings for me legs. As I was tellin' the others, by the time I leave, I'll either be fit or dead.' She laughs. Kim gives a formal smile, brushes her fringe from her face. She turns to face Crilly.

'Well, it's been a while.'

'Aye.' They embrace stiffly. The other visitors leave in a clump. Siobhan cringes visibly at those who kiss her cheek. It is just the four of us now. Kim gives me a smile of allegiance. 'How exotic you are,' she says. I blush, though the compliment pleases.

The door bursts open again, with a kind of clatter. A tall, broad-shouldered Amazonian woman towers above us, a sweet-faced, blond-haired man in her tow.

'Crilly, by Jaz, me dashing broter. Will you look at yourself, ya' posh bastard!' She throws her arms about Crilly's neck. He reciprocates, beaming.

'What about you, Megan. You're lookin' grand. Your hair is so long!'

'Aye, I'm a real woman now. Will you say hello to Peter?' Peter shuffles to the fore, takes Crilly's hand, pats his shoulder. Megan pushes to the edge of Siobhan's bed. 'How are ye' Mam?'

'Well, as I was tellin' the others, I'll either be fit or dead by the time I get out of here.'

'Rubbish, you're strong as a harse, I tell you!' Megan's jaw is strong, her cheekbones high, her eyes loud and blue and busy. Her tawny hair falls to her shoulders in an even crop. As I have heard that Kim is the beauty of the family, Lorraine the sensible one, and Megan the tomboy, I am surprised by the strength of Megan's face, the magnificent width of features, the flush of her skin. When she looks at me, I shrink.

'Megan,' says Siobhan, 'this is Claudia Coe, Crilly's girlfriend from America.'

'I figured it out for meself, Mam.' Megan holds out her hand. 'Did he tell you what a bastard I am?' she asks me.

'Not at all.'

From the corner of the room, Kim clears her throat. Megan looks up but does not move. 'How're ye' keepin', Kimberly?'

'I'm fine. You're looking well.'

'Been exercisin', you know. Twice round the block after gettin' the little ones to school.'

'It shows.'

'Just a little.'

Peter shuffles forth to meet me. Relieved by his mildness, I take his hand.

Megan and Peter take us to their local. It is a squat and arid room of swirly carpet, above a shop. The place is empty but for the bar and three or four slightly-built lads shooting pool without words. While Crilly asks Peter about his postman job, Megan fills me in on Kimberly's scandal.

'When Kimberley divorced her husband and made off wi' t' other, Lorraine and she fell out and you could say I was fumin' as well. Tere was tree young children involved, you know. Horrible names we called each other. Whore. Traitor. Jaz I can't bear to say tem. Lorraine never went to Kim's second wedding. Tey still don't speak. It's mad — even Mum's after botering w' it now.'

'And you?'

'Ah me? well, me, I'm neutral, you know.'

Peter and Crilly and Megan drink many glasses of Guinness. I can't stomach it. I like the sweet easy syrup of Tia Maria, but dread the quizzical glance of the barman whenever I order it.

'You look like that French actress,' I tell Megan, after I have switched to Bloody Mary, 'Marie-Christine Barrault.'

'Now who the fock's that?'

'A French actress. You look like her.'

'Is that good now?'

'Yes, she's beautiful.'

Megan turns to face her husband.

'Peter, did you hear tha'? I look like Mary Burry, what te' . . . what was that name?' She turns back to me.

'Marie-Christine Barrault.' I repeat.

'Aye, Marie Christiane . . . some film star. The French one.'

Megan asks me questions.

'You're from Hollywood people yourself, are you?' she asks.

'Well sort of. Behind the scenes, really.'

'But your Da' invented soap operas? Like *Inferno's Village*?'

'That's right.'

'So why are you not over 'tere, bein' some kind of movie star, rather than sittin' in a pub in Santry, in the middle of autumn ta' feels like winter?'

I think about this. 'I prefer it on this side of the sea,' I say at last, and I mean it, though I can't quite remember which sea I'm talking about.

As we walk out to our cars, Peter shuffles in beside me, telling me about his children. Megan pushes forward to bid me farewell.

'You'll have to excuse me husband,' she says, 'he get's a bit borin' after a few pints.' She hugs me. 'Let me tell you, chicken. Before I first met ye' right, I expected to fockin' hate you.'

'Oh?'

'Aye, well you know, rich tiny 'ting from those United States, all ta' money and breedin' and such. But in the hospital you were smilin' like and I knew I was mistakin'. Me broter's found a gem in you. And he's lookin' grand himself, not pinned or stoned or nuttin'. Seems you've done a good job with our Crilly.'

In bed I lie.

'They think I'm straight.'

'And why wouldn't they?'

'Because I'm not.'

'To them you are. You're not emaciated, you don't have track marks, you look like a million.'

'That's only make-up. I'm white as anything.'

Crilly turns onto his side.

'Crilly?' I whisper.

But Crilly is silent.

There is only one methadone clinic in Dublin. It looks remarkably similar to the one in London; the same pamphlets scarring the walls, the hard tile floor, an old copy of *Mother's World* upon the table. The patients, too, are the same; skinny single parents in stone-washed jeans, hair longish and limp with bleach, oily-haired lads in dirty anoraks, babies in prams and famished couples. The only difference is that there are more children, children everywhere, playing with torn-haired dolls and metal trucks upon the floor and vinyl seats.

In the afternoon, we visit a friend of Crilly's from childhood. The friend is called Bobby and he lives in a slum near the city centre. We drive there on an empty street which is barely rubble, strewn with rusty cans that look like tankers, sweet wrappers, empty beer bottles and hordes of children shouting by the side of the road. A brawny, brown-faced old man looks as though his face has been squashed by a rock. He stands before our car.

'Shit.' I say. The man scowls at us, slitting his eyes. He makes his way to Crilly's window.

'Crilly Lynch, ya' big bastard, are ye' slummin' it or wot?' Crilly laughs and shakes his hand. 'What about you, Murphy? We're after your son!'

'You're a lyin' cunt, Crilly. Ye' be makin' trouble as in te' old days, wi' yer shiny motor and yer' posh girlfriend. Showin' off, I should imagine!'

'Can't argue with you there, Murphy.'

'Not ta' I blame ye, mind. Your man's lazin' at home as he always is.'

''Tanks, Murphy.'

'It's grand te' see ye', man. And the auld dear's chattin' to Bernice just a' te corner there. She'll be wantin' to see ye.'

'Aye, of course.'

At the corner we stop to say hello to Bobby's mother, a weathered woman with a big head, wearing a tartan apron. She stands squarely with her hands on her hips the whole time, beaming at Crilly and remarking often upon the colour of the sky.

'At least we've got dacent wet'er for ye, Crilly. The silver sun has takin' well to yer visitin'.'

And so it has, for the broken pavement is blinding white with sunshine. The methadone is beginning to take effect. I think the street is very beautiful.

Bobby, gay and slender and handsome, has always lived in the ghetto. He rents a room above a hairdresser's. He has a trendy haircut and wears a dangling earring, but his accent is like his father's. He is delighted to see Crilly, and extends a hearty handshake to myself. He apologises for the mess and sets to work clearing books and bottles and brochures off the one cracked settee for us to sit on.

'Really, don't bother yourself, Bobby,' says Crilly.

'No bot'er. Claudia, you may want to be checkin' yer motor every minute or so. Them hooligans won't spare 'temselves for no friend of mine.'

'They still bothering you Bobby?' asks Crilly, concerned.

'Too bloody right. 'Tem bastards go on queerbashin' tirades

at every opportunity. Lucky for me 'tey won't touch me, as I've got me family, just down te' road.'

'Aye, you're family's a fierce faithful bunch.'

'Even at fifty-five, not a soul with sense in his head will go near me Da'.'

'He's a good man, your Da'.'

'He's a drunkin' auld bigot. Just last week he beat bloody hell out of some old tramp all legless like and pissed over himself. He just put it to the poor bastard. I do like him, mind.'

I look out of the window at my car, but it is really the street I am interested in. Identical grey tenements line the road like toothless mouths with windows missing, windows broken. The corner is vacant but for several ancient vehicles robbed of tyres and glass, propped up on petrol cans and boulders. Five or six teenagers loiter in front of a newsagent, drinking shandy and smoking. The methadone is hitting hard; I am dizzy. I warned Crilly that 40ml was too much to ask for, and I was right. He doesn't believe me. He is full of chat now, feeling fine, gossiping to Bobby about old friends, his eyes bright and pinned; his eyes are like twins who are also friends. I sit down and Bobby thrusts a gold-rimmed album into my arms, in which there are old photos of Crilly, Megan, Maggie and other people whom I do not know but have heard about. As much as I try to enjoy the album, I am overcome with nausea. The old photos of Maggie, straight and young and demure though she looks, make it worse.

Driving home is a dangerous chore. From the inner-city I steer shakily over the Liffey and through the cobbled streets and mixed primary colours of old Dublin, through a wide stretch of bleak, bland suburbs and onto a motorway. The urgency of nausea brings me to Siobhan's house without difficulty and, once there, I crumble to my knees and vomit into the toilet, after which I fall headlong into bed and sleep for three or four hours.

When I awake, the sickness has gone, but the high has remained and I feel fitter than I have done in the whole of our visit. Crilly comes to my bedside with a neatly prepared square of foil and a tube, and I suck from it happily. Crilly cups my face in his hands, strokes my hair and kisses me long upon the lips.

'Who do you belong to?' he asks sweetly.

'You and the devil.'

'Everyone thinks you're beautiful.'

'Good.'

'And so you are. I've just spoken to Megan. After visiting me auld dear, we'll meet the others at Kimberly's house for a late supper.'

'Lovely.'

'This is a great novelty, you know. Lorraine and Kim and Megan haven't been in the same house together since Kim was married.'

'Will it be strange?'

'I don't know. Accidents do funny things to people.'

Siobhan is alone in her room today, watching a documentary about English people who eat moths. She seems lively, her bed strewn with magazines and a pint glass of 7-UP by her side, reminding me of myself in childhood, when I stayed home from school with flu, drinking flat 7-UP, eating Saltines. Her Marks and Spencer coat has been recovered from the accident and it is draped across the foot of her bed, as though she is fixing to leave.

'Ah, Crilly,' she says, as we walk through the door, 'you're late. Jimmy Shawn was askin' for you.'

'Who?' Crilly sits down by the window and opens a gardening magazine.

'Now don't be pretendin' you don't know who he is! Paddy Shawn's boy. Used to work at the laundry in Bonner Street. You knew him well when you were small.'

'Oh. Well I'm not small, now.' Crilly turns the pages of his magazine.

'As if I couldn't see for meself. Anyway, Jimmy's engaged. To some seamstress girl from Skibbereen. They're to be married in May in Dingle.'

'Why Dingle?'

'Her people are there. They've invited you to the wedding.'

'Yes, I've been meaning to get down to Dingle.'

'Don't be makin' fon now! You 'tink you're too good for Dingle!'

'Dingle's too good for me.'

Siobhan rolls her eyes. 'He's sure gettin' full of London airs. Dingle's a lovely place. I spent me honeymoon there.'

Crilly is intent on his gardening magazine.

'Anyway,' persists Siobhan, 'Jimmy's an enterprisin' fellow these days. He's opening a co-op market in the south side. Not that you're the least bit interested.'

Crilly does not reply. He is suddenly a sullen youth, a petulant teenager. I want to hit him. Siobhan turns her attention to me.

'Do you believe in God?' she asks. Crilly looks up. I swallow.

'I'm sorry?'

'Do you believe in God?' Her eyes are so clear, I cannot shuffle nor stray from the beam of them.

'Well . . .' I stutter, searching for the words, 'not in the strict sectarian sense . . . I was raised, you know, as an atheist, or really as an agnostic . . . God is . . . I mean my ancestry is so confused . . . I mean, I believe in some force, but we make our own destiny . . . I've always been intrigued by the Catholic church, by all the colours and the candles, but I know so little about it . . . when we studied existentialism in high school, I felt that that was exactly right, but now I just don't know . . . I mean, such strange things happen.'

Siobhan smiles. 'Aye, they do.'

'I suppose . . . I suppose . . . I would really like to believe.'

'Aye.'

I expect her to say more, to preach or pose a second question, but she doesn't. She leans back on her headrest. As we stand to leave, she takes the hand of her son.

'Crilly,' she whispers, loud enough for me to hear, 'she's a lovely girl.'

We make our way down the corridor, saying nothing.

Unlike her sisters, Kimberly lives in a rural cottage twenty miles outside of the city. We take the narrow country road and we are low on fuel. The night is black and there are no streetlights, and I feel as though I am not driving on a road at all, but forcing my way through clotted bushes. I am afraid of many things; that we will run out of petrol, that we will get lost amidst the velvety nowhere, that my slug of an engine will give way at last and abandon us to our own feebleness. I am relieved when we reach the drive of Kim's house, pebble-paved, warmly lit. And I am not too tired, not too stoned and not too straight.

Contrasting considerably from the Spartan angularity of Siobhan's bungalow, Kim's house reminds me of American homes I have seen, lavish with plum and antiques to imitate English country homes. Handel is playing on the CD and candles are lit, and the most beautiful children I have ever seen scurry about in pink and cream pyjamas. Kim meets us at the door wearing a shimmering dress. Her husband, Martin, is a husky, pipe-smoking, grey-haired man with a handlebar moustache, sitting broadly in his armchair, homey and smug. Megan and Peter crunch together on the settee, both wearing jeans and gulping glasses of wine and saying nothing. Their own four children are stuffed between them. Immediately after we have seated ourselves, Kim's sons and daughters come to us like honeyed fairies, gazing amorously into our eyes and asking questions about where we have come from and would we like to see their rooms. Martin sends them off to bed, despite our protests.

Lorraine and her husband Cal are the last to arrive. Cal is a dark and intense-looking man, and he has a guitar. Cal and Lorraine accept drinks, Megan's button-faced little ones slither off to watch television, and the eight of us sit drinking and lost for conversation, once the civilities of work and children and Siobhan's condition have been done with. Kim spends most of her time in the kitchen, charting the progress of her late supper. I am drawn to Cal's guitar, and I finally cannot help but ask if he will play a tune, something by Christy Moore. Cal embarks upon a soporific rendition of 'I'm An Ordinary Man'. I know many of the words, and I sing along with the others. When he is done, I ask if he will play 'Carrickfergus'. He groans at this. 'You Americans always go for the corny ones,' he says, but he plays it just the same, and he delivers a good strong solo at that. When he is done, Megan requests 'The Knock', on behalf of Siobhan's recent fiasco. We all know the words to this one.

> At the early age of thirty-eight me mother sent me West
> Get up, said she, and get a job says I I'll do me best
> I pulled on my Wellingtons to march to march to Kiljimock
> But I took a wrong turn at Charlestown and ended up in
>   Knock
> Once this quiet crossroads was a place of quiet prayer
> Where Catholics got indulgent once or twice a year
> You could buy a pair of rosary beads or get your candles
>   blessed
> If you had a guilty conscience, you could get it off your
>   chest . . .

Cal wants me to sing a song. I refuse, but after much heckling from the others, I agree to sing 'Nancy Spain', if Cal will accompany me. He does, treading slowly as I am uncertain of the words though in fact I do know them, having memorised them like a nursery rhyme. Despite my nervousness, I sing it well and receive a hearty applause at the end. Our limbs loosened by good wine and song and the penetrating aroma of simmering chicken, we sing for the rest of the night, breaking only to eat. I am ecstatic. This is the Celtic family I have always longed for, complete with live fires, family feuds, squirming freckle-nosed children a-playing in the next room, suggestive sighing and eyeing between the sisters, the indisputable unity created by the sick mother/grandmother in hospital, the indisputable union of songs you always know whether you want to remember them or not. Even Perry knows them. Even Crilly knows them. I flash upon my own family; the way I have to think a moment before deciding who to include in my family, whether to include the step-parents or the siblings on my father's side whom I would not know should I see them on the street, the hastiness of Mom and Larry on Sunday swirls between galleries and sushi, untapered by excess or sentimentality, busy with books and foreign films and the Sunday supplement of the *New York Times*, the wisdom of Ivy Leagues and schedules too dense to live by, to wake by, to sleep and breathe by. There are no perimeters in that world that I can feel; I am a trick of their fate, peripheral, unclassy, bored.

We sing. I could live here, I could live in this place forever, and neither here nor there would blink an eye.

It is four a.m. Crilly is plastered. With my help, he makes his way up the steep stairwell to the bedroom, though the covers are slacken to him and he has no hope of getting beneath them. He regains his strength when I sit upon the bed beside him; he reaches for me, he kisses me violently. I recoil at the strength of his putrid breath and yank myself away, but he grabs my waist and throws me upon the bed, pinning my hands down and forcing himself on top of me. Queasy from 40ml and smack and so much wine, his stench makes me want to vomit. I spit in his face. He slaps me and I swear at him, growling now, guttural. He tears my knickers and thrusts his hand inside me, and I hit him, hard. He rolls off me and passes out on the pillow, the smell of his drunkenness lingering like something live. He begins to snore. His heaving shakes the entire bed. I retreat to the bathroom and vomit. I stagger to the bedroom and pull out the cover from beneath him. I leave the room and the light on, bare and ugly, just for spite.

The guest bedroom is a small room with a tiny window, and it has nothing in it but a single bed, a lamp on a nightstand and Jesus hanging, plain and formidable, above the bed, I sit above the covers, staring into space. I do this for a long time. I have no sensation of hours, minutes, seconds. My head and nose congest with the smell of toothpaste and vomit. (Even my vision seems rank like the gelling of sour milk.) Slumber does not take me. I see only the face of Siobhan, lovely and awake in her hospital bed, her introductions and information, her Jimmy Shawns, her Rorys and Frankie Mulligans and Patsy McCauleys, and her words, Do you believe, do you believe in God? I see me in my shame, the horror of this hour; mascara fallout littering my face like ashes, my skin dank with the sweat of Crilly and myself, my underwear torn and hanging from my hips, and me, small and stoned and sobbing, beneath the stern emphatic white of Siobhan's cross.

search

Our return drive from Holyhead is peppered by queasy naps at
service stations, the shuffle of luggage thumping at our backs,
and intermittent searches for Crilly's acid tabs which have been
lost somewhere along the way. In Dublin, Crilly bought four
six-foot posters from the Sinn Fein bookshop, taking up the
length of the car's interior, rolling back and forth and jutting
into our chins like restless pets. They block the rear view of the
road and make our quest to recover the tabs all the more
difficult. The posters shout in bold slogans in yellow and orange
letters with shadowy figures of fire and guns, gunmen hovering
over hillsides, burning buildings beneath.

I am secretly relieved at the loss of the acid, for not only do I
dislike hallucinogens, but I fear we will be stopped, yet another
time, by the police. But Crilly says he needs the money he
should have gotten for them in Dublin. He does not fear police
pursuit. Not for the drugs, anyway. He says we have more to fear
from the posters. Less than a fortnight ago, the IRA bombed
army barracks in Kent. Nearing Birmingham, Crilly grows
maudlin. He talks about the Birmingham Six. It's all right for
you, he tells me, with your middle class accent and your
American passport. They'd never take you for a terrorist.

Then why buy posters? I ask. He doesn't reply. The drive
takes twelve hours in all.

At home we make a promise to ourselves. We will not smoke
heroin ever again. We have generous methadone prescriptions

under pseudonyms. It is an opportunity to pack it in, to make our leap from smack to medication, from medication to cleanliness. Firm in our resolution, we keep our weekly appointments to UCH clinic, show clean urine on our tests, and visit the chemist daily. Crilly gets a job raising curtains at a West End theatre and I become a barmaid at a busy Soho pub. I am functional on the methadone; I can stand to get out of bed before three in the afternoon, I write poetry and draw from time to time, and even manage to socialise a little, dining at an occasional restaurant, catching the odd play. Things are looking up. The shelf above the television is cluttered with empty methadone bottles bearing our pseudonyms. I don't know why we don't throw them away; perhaps we are charting our progress.

I am alone in the flat when the buzzer shrills one soggy afternoon. It is five o'clock in winter; the sky steams with night. The heat is on full blast. I am hot and listless; I wear sweats and my hair is pulled from my face with a rubber band. I speak into the entry system.

'It's Brendan,' says Crilly, giving his pseudonym, 'with the Old Bill. No joke.'

I run downstairs. I shove my hash and papers into a bookshelf. I assume that Crilly has been picked up on one of his many 'wanted' charges and that the police are calling to confirm the address he has given. It's happened before. He gets off, usually. I open the front door. Crilly stands handcuffed amongst six policemen; only one looks older than he is. The older one steps forward.

'Claudia Coe?'

'Yes.'

'We have arrested your boyfriend, Brendan McNally, for possession of hashish and two tabs of LSD, found on his person on Camden Lock, NW1. Subsequently we have reason to believe that he is keeping additional narcotics on the premises and we have a right to search your home without a warrant.'

I look at Crilly. He nods. I stand back and let them in. They make for the stairwell with Crilly firmly in hand, blasting upwards like stiff navy rockets. My one advantage is that they do not know the layout of the flat. The flat is large. I run to the bedroom, clutch the lump of hash from the bookshelf, and lock myself in the bathroom, turning the taps on. I flush the lot down the toilet, staring at myself in the mirror, trembling. When I emerge, a young copper is standing outside.

'What are you doing?' he asks. He has a Scottish accent. His head is narrow, his features pointy.

'Going to the loo.'

'Why did you not go before we came?'

'I didn't have to go then. I always have to go when I'm nervous.'

The copper pushes his way into the bathroom, scrutinizes the sink and toilet. He finds nothing. I edge away from him.

'Where do you think you're going?'

'Upstairs, with my boyfriend.'

His eyes are narrow on mine. 'How do I know you haven't flushed something down there?'

'I haven't, I promise,' I try to stop the quivering. 'I'm just frightened. I've never had my place searched before.'

'Perhaps it would be wise to search you?' he asks, almost politely, as though it were not a rhetorical question.

I back away. He comes closer. I start to cry. The copper stares at me and speaks into his static machine, spouting some code number and a location.

'Get a policewoman here as soon as you can,' he says. 'I've got a lassie here that I just don't trust.' When he finishes with the machine, he replaces it upon his hip. 'Come with me,' he says, 'I don't want you out of my sight.'

I slowly ascend the stairs, the copper behind me. Crilly sits in the living-room, cuffed to a cop beside him, watching the others as they tear through the shelves. My shelves. One of them frisks a large steel ashtray and hands a roach to another.

'There's a bit of a spliff anyway,' he says. The second policeman lowers it into a plastic bag. I sit beside Crilly on the footrest. He puts his free arm around me and I hide my face in his chest.

'Don't be frightened,' he murmurs, 'I'm the one who's been nicked. Don't cry. I love you. Don't cry.'

'No whispering!' shouts a thin, quick copper. He's young, this one, no more than twenty, and he wears street clothes, a yellow nylon shirt. His hair is black and parted on the side. His voice is a shriek, high-pitched cockney.

'I'm not whispering!' yells Crilly. 'Me girlfriend's frightened. I'm consoling her.'

Another policeman, fat and in uniform, comes forward and sticks his baton between us, separating us. He stares down at Crilly. His moustache shines with sweat.

'I wouldn't be so cheeky, Paddy,' he says in a low voice. 'You're in a lot of trouble. You and your bird. Though what she's doing with a thick Irish cunt like you is beyond me.'

The plain-clothed cockney sidles up to the moustached man, grinning.

'You're more trouble than the Wogs. You Dublin geezers are so bent, you can't even lie in bed straight!'

I wonder if they will hit him. But their movements are narrow, controlled. The yellow shirt looks at me.

'Any progress with that policewoman?' he asks the Scot.

'No,' replies the Scot, who is busy pulling ornaments from the shelves, examining them, breaking them. 'None available just now.' He holds up a wooden multi-coloured fish. 'What's this, Spanish?' he asks me.

'Mexican.'

'Very nice. Went there on me honeymoon, with the wife. Very hot.' He breaks the fish in two.

The two coppers ease off and rip up the carpet.

'Should I offer them a cup of tea?' I whisper to Crilly.

Crilly laughs, almost. He pulls me close and tells me to sit tight.

'No whispering!' shouts the moustached man. They divide us. Three of them stay upstairs with Crilly, while the other three ask me to show them the bedroom. We pass through the foyer. The Sinn Fein posters stand rolled and erect against the wall. I flash on the special branch: sleepless interrogations in window-less cells. Crilly is right; drugs are nothing compared to this. We proceed into the bedroom. I sit upon the bed, holding myself with my arms, while the coppers empty drawers, shelves, closets. The oldest one sits beside me. He is balding and pleasant-faced, like a father.

'You see love,' he says, 'LSD is a Class A drug. Sort of a drug felony. Did you know that?'

I shake my head. The plain-clothed cockney ransacks my underwear drawer, sticking his hand into bras and panties. He finds a letter at the bottom and reads it. I cannot remember who the letter is from. The moustached man opens a cabinet door. We are all silent in the face of sixty empty methadone bottles.

'What's that?' he asks.

'I haven't a clue.' My mind blanks.

The copper reads the name on the bottles.

'Who's Kathleen McGuire?'

'You'll have to ask Cri — Brendan.'

I hear a scuffle as the others tear down the stairs to search the study. Crilly keeps his illegal dole cards in the study. Five or six of them, all in a carrier bag, all under different names. This is his primary livelihood. I prepare myself to lose him for years and years.

'Surely, he's not Kathleen McGuire,' he turns to face me. 'Are you a junkie?'

'No.'

'Do you smoke hashish?'

'No.'

He leans down, squatting before me. 'You can tell me,' he says confidentally. 'Hash isn't such a big deal. We've even tried it; the lads and I. Everyone does it.'

I shake my head.

'What are you doing with all those methadone bottles?'

'They're not mine.'

'And if your boyfriend says they are?'

'He wouldn't say that.'

'Is Brendan a junkie?'

I am silent. The moustached man leans closer. 'I've seen your boyfriend, your Brendan, in a great many shady places. Only it seems they was callin' him by a different name, or names even. Brendan. Patsy. Crilly. Shamus. Paddy names, the lot. You're American, 'nt you?'

I nod.

'Are you here legally?'

'Yes, I'm a student.'

'No problems with immigration?'

'Of course not.'

The moustached man opens his palm, presenting me with an old square of foil, streaked with dry runs of smack. 'I found this under the bed.'

I shake my head, I bury my face, I deny all knowledge of the silver foil. He tells me I'm a stupid girl, that all the posh solicitors in Beverly Hills can't get me out of Holloway on a drug charge.

'Leave her alone, Mark,' says the fatherly cop, putting his hand on mine. 'It's him we want. We've got him.' He leans down and looks into my eyes. 'Listen, love, we're not really interested in old foil or empty bottles or roaches. We have reason to believe that your boyfriend is in possession of a considerable amount of LSD. You can make things easier for us.'

'How?' I sniff.

'You can tell us a bit about him. About his friends. We know he's a heroin addict. Heroin's a nasty drug. It may be no time at all before he's got you in the racket. I wouldn't want that for you.'

The moustached man hits the top bookshelf. 'What are all these notebooks?' he asks.

'They're for my writing class,' I say. Years before, I did telephone sex with Pamela, from a musty office in Baron's Court. We kept records of every client, including where he lived and what his preferences were. We kept our notes in plain notebooks bound in black. I can see them now, standing in the middle of the shelf, amidst college journals, old diaries. The moustached man begins to read aloud from an old diary. The copper reads,

'The morning is hell. I'm too fucked up to walk. I hate the sky. I feel like shit. That prick Davy Mulligan's stiffed us with brown sugar . . .'

He looks up at me, his brow arched in prurient scowl. As he goes on to the next, I glance at his fingers. I don't care about the diaries. I'm praying he'll somehow miss the phone stuff.

The fatherly cop asks if I plan to cooperate . . .

'I don't know anything,' I say. 'I'm in my last year of art school. I don't take drugs. I don't even drink.'

'We never said we minded if you drink.'

'But I don't.'

'Drink is legal.'

'I know.'

The moustached man reads aloud. 'Mr Carnegie, Aberdeen. Likes to have cock sucked. Fancies being tied down by redheaded schoolgirl beneath billiards table. Likes watching Jeanette fuck black boxer resembling Frank Bruno in airplane . . .'

That's the one. The fatherly cop is disappointed in me. I can tell.

'That's for your writing class?' Again, the moustached man.

'It's research. For an article I was doing on telephone sex.' The yellow shirt orders me off the bed and tears through the sheets. He finds nothing. He brings his face close to mine.

'The people I have to deal with,' he says. 'The scumbags. The retrogrades. The whores . . .' He turns to face the elder policeman.

'What's the matter with you?' he asks.

'I don't think "retrograde" is the right word.'

'Well, what is it then?'

'I don't know . . . reprobate, perhaps?' The third copper nods. Not to be upstaged, the yellow shirt returns to me. '. . . I know you, love. You're the worse kind of scum. At least with your paddy, we can see the dirt. With you, it hides beneath. It's all very well for you, with your posh flat, your Habitat duvet. But you, you're devious. A liar. You're a devious liar.'

He's so close I think he'll touch me. I sidle up to the older cop.

The moustached man points to the word processor. 'And how do we know that everything in this dump hasn't fallen off the back of a lorry?'

The fatherly cop intercepts.

'Leave it out, Mark.' He looks at me. 'You'll be all right. We know you're not to blame.'

'Like hell!' shouts the yellow shirt. 'Her Sloanie mates will be visiting her in prison if I have anything to do with it.'

Suddenly, he is absurd to me, like something out of *The Bill*. I am dizzy, it feels very late. My eyes glaze over, my muscles go limp. 'I don't know anything,' I repeat with exaggerated lethargy. The others crop up at the door, holding Crilly.

'We've got it!' announces the Scot. I brace myself for the sight of the posters, unrolled and exposed, and the dole cards.

But it is the acid he holds, a hundred tabs of it. An open copy of Nell McAfferty lies helplessly in the doorway.

'Nice one, Greg!' chortles the yellow shirt, folding a bra and putting it back in the drawer. Reflexively, I tell him to leave it; I will do it. As fast as they came, the assembly gathers and rushes us towards the door. The yellow shirt stops and hands me a plastic carrier bag containing the soiled foil, the roaches and the methadone bottles, compartmentalised in bags like specimens.

'Get rid of this, love,' he says. 'We're letting you off easy this time. But we'll be back. We can get a warrant to search your place at any time. So look after your rubbish, if you know what I mean!'

The fatherly copper smiles at me. 'Get yourself a nice bloke, Claudia,' he advises. At the sound of my name I jump a little. 'You're wasting your time with this one.' I stand in the early darkness and watch as Crilly is bundled into the back of the red and white van and taken away, siren silent but the bright lights flashing.

pentonville

It is no surprise to me when he is caught. With his clammy hands and his face furrowed at nothing more than the flap of pigeons' wings or the sight of a meter maid, he seemed to be waiting for it. He does not share my talent for deceit, the agility of lies.

But I wish it hadn't been tonight, for tonight we have been invited to Gemma's house for supper. And the flat sparkled before the rampage; a place to return to, a home for afterwards. For beans on toast at midnight or the Late Show in bed. Crilly never saw it so clean. He hung his head and crooked his elbow, conceding to the cuffs, waiting for the mess to be made. It was inevitable, I know. We both knew.

Now that the troops are gone, I sit back on the *chaise-longue*, that Japanese fish-tailed thing, and close the fan beside me, blocking the street and the living-room. I sit and stare for some time, wondering if he is sick.

He phones at nine, from the local cells at Kentish Town. He tells me to meet him at the magistrates' court the following morning, tells me to keep away from the scumbags. To stay inside and keep warm. To eat something nourishing and to sleep.

Behind him there are voices, growing closer, louder; the static of a walkie-talkie, an irate officer.

He has to go now, he says. 'I love you Claudia, I hanker for you now, already, kitten, Jezebel. I'll think of your body tonight to warm my cell. Christ and how I really love you.'

The words seem unreal. Not just his words, but my own, not spoken or thought, just lingering somewhere, dormant. Like pulses in your ear when you're so tired that your skin is pudding and all sounds are amplified and irritable in bulk.

I wonder how I am physically. Am I hungry? I couldn't eat. Do I want to buy more hash, a chunky offering for my wicker mini-basket? No, it will make me dizzy, my thinking unclear. There's only one thing I really want. But I don't know the dealers, other than Perry, who wastes away now in Karachi. Crilly took care of the gear, he took care of everything. I am as an invalid housewife, unresourceful and unknowing, who leaves business to her husband. Waits at the foot of her bed watching *Home and Away*, waiting for the goods to arrive. Waiting for something to look forward to. I don't want to know the dealers. They probably wouldn't serve me anyway; little rich girl on the hill, her friends 'dabble' in the arts and they don't take smack and neither does she, really, except on weekends. Or so they think. Maybe. No tracks. Crilly's easy ride. O fuck. I don't really know what they think, or if they think, or if they give a shit about any of it in any case.

I don't dare to visit the methadone clinic tomorrow. It's too dangerous. I'd rather be sick. I *will* be sick tomorrow. It won't be too bad; my habit is small. Smaller than his. A day, perhaps. And I then I will be clean! I thrill at the novelty. But will I sleep at night?

I go to Gemma's as planned. I bring a bottle of Spanish wine. I could walk but instead I drive.

The house is newly furnished with tasteful things. A plump settee stands against the mantel, turquoise. A sleek, low coffee table. Polished floorboards and a South American rug. Three deep-seated armchairs, blazing red. The fireplace chequered with old Dutch tiles. A roaring fire. I think regretfully of my own fireplace; I have not had the chimney-sweep around; it can't be used. It would have been so *easy* to have the chimney-sweep around.

Several of Gemma's paintings adorn the walls. Great big colourful things; jubilant with primary colours. Five or six people I've never met lounge discreetly in chairs with their legs crossed, or spread themselves upon the floor, clutching their knees. They are from St Martin's College of Art. The women wear short black skirts and black tights. One has a tidy French bob and oversized silver hoops in her ears. Another has her hair cut in a short crop, dyed a deep pink. Her earrings are long, falling almost to her shoulders, strands of tiny men and women climbing the chrome pieces of an antique watch. I like the earrings very much. We eat cheese and rice crackers from a platter on the coffee table, and in the kitchen, Stewart, Gemma's fiancé, prepares supper on his new sushi-making machine.

Gemma is only nineteen. Stewart is twenty-one. He is a talent scout. He finds bands to dance to. He is tall and thin with mousey-coloured hair, long on one side. Gemma sits like a reclining obelisk with messy hair dyed a shade lighter than his, large eyes resting at an artful slant, a full mouth. She speaks with a London accent, though her father knows the Royal Family. Gemma is one of the few prosperous people I know in London, other than myself. In company, we both complain of debts and overdrafts, cringing from our easy parental money. When it is only the two of us, however, we discuss gifts we are given, exotic restaurants in which we have dined. Stewart is the opposite of Gemma; a working-class lad from Dagenham who speaks the Queen's English. He speaks publicly of motorbikes and holidays he will take to Australia, Borneo, Malaysia. Aesthetically, they are a pleasing couple.

I sit on the floor beside the art student with the pink hair. She is called Bernadette and she is from Newcastle. Her eyes are the keenest green I have ever seen as though they, too, have been dyed. Her face is a perfect circle. Her lips share the pink of her hair. She reminds me of marionettes I have seen. As I settle into my piece of floor, she adjusts herself and smiles at me.

'I've heard your name mentioned,' she says, her voice high, her accent only slightly northern. 'Are you Italian?'

'No, I'm American.'

'You don't sound it.'

'Do I sound Italian?'

'No. You look Italian.'

'Is that good?'

'Aye! My cousin married an Italian girl called Francesca. She looks a bit like you.'

'I've always wanted to be called Francesca.'

'My friend from boarding-school is called Claudia. She's American. Is Claudia an American name?'

'I don't think so. It's rather generic.'

'You sound English.'

'Well, I have a bit of an identity complex.'

'You don't want to be English, do you?'

'Not really. I'd rather be Apache.'

'Then why don't you live in New Mexico?'

'It's too hot.'

'You look like you could be part-Apache.'

'No, I'm mostly Lithuanian.'

'I thought you were American?'

'We're all from somewhere else.'

'Except, of course, if you're Apache.'

'This is very true.'

I am exhausted. I could ask to borrow the bedroom to sleep for awhile. Instead I ask Bernadette about art college. Gemma comes into the room, tiptoeing to avoid ashtrays and guests. She carries a plate of seaweed things. We eat. Someone called

Sebastian says that he has named the movement to follow post-modernism; it is called belatedness. I try not to clutch my pelvis, down there where the rot is.

'Where's Crilly?' asks Gemma.

'He's at Holborn Station.'

'What's he doing there?'

'He's going to prison.'

Silence. I eat seaweed.

'It's weird to eat seaweed,' I say. 'I've been eating it for years but it's weird. You know when you're small, you cover yourself with ropes of it and run along the beach? Till you get all slimy and wet? It feels weird to eat it.'

Gemma laughs. She is good to me. Her friends exchange glances. I ask about the wedding.

Sebastian says he will get it on video. I excuse myself and stand in the bathroom and stare at my reflection. My hair is flat, it has lost its curl. My skin is translucent, as though it were a pond, with a straining surface of pink at its bottom. My eyes are without light, except for the glass of the day's methadone. My nose shines. I want to go home. Instead, I return to the living-room and try to think about art.

I'm grateful to sleep soundly. I awake at seven, amazed at myself, and bathe and dress in a bright colour. I ride the tube to Bond Street and walk easily to the courthouse. I feel pleasant as I go, pleased at the newness of a crowded centre at a civilised hour, cleansed by the cheery flush of early morning. At Great Marlborough Street, Crilly is tired, wearing a T-shirt of mine and short trousers he wore yesterday. He will not tell the magistrate where he lives. He is protecting me. The magistrate gives him a three-week remand in custody. The brief is a fat effeminate, dead-eyed man. As Crilly is taken back into the cells, he catches my eyes. He shrugs. It is a beginning for both of us. Cleanliness. Routine. I come away from the courthouse, brushing slowly through the streets, gazing at Liberty's and the Haunch of Venison Avenue. I am without the sense of purpose that woke me so early. My body is lazy like loose yarn, but I'm not sick yet. What is heroin anyway, but a dark shadow, a temporary respite, smoked between one and a few hundred times? Suck on a tube and smooch a bit, talk about childhood in a sleepy voice. Listen to the Ink Spots, watch *Paris, Texas* for the eighth or ninth time, shut the doors and lie back on those same damp pillows. (The big ones, from that little shop in Tufnell Park.) What could it be but powder, poppies? It will not leave me too sick, it will not punish me too much. It isn't cancer.

I'm a three-year-old who hates shots and squeezes her eyes tight at the sight of a needle. I'm not a junkie. My boyfriend was an altar boy. I won't be left in ruins. I have endured a phase of my adulthood, a crucial phase. It's over now and I deserve a rest. I take a taxi home.

I strip the sheets and remake the bed with bedclothes which, while not altogether clean, are at least fresh with the cool of unuse. I roll a joint and fall into bed with my remote control. I smoke my spliff and switch on the telly; I am just in time for *Neighbours*. Eventually sleep comes.

Throughout the day, the telephone rings. I do not answer, nor do I open my eyes, but I am stirred by the relentless bleep and static of the answerphone; words, artificial like a megaphone, filtering through.

Crilly, phone me, will you, it's Maggie.

Crilly, won't you ring me, I must talk to you.

Claudia, if you see Crilly, please tell him I called.

Crilly it's Maggie; Seamus was asking for you, where the hell are you?

Where the fuck are you Crilly!

Where the fuck are you? FUCK. Fuck. My eyelids flickering and then squeezed tense. Her voice is shrill with urgency, it riots in the dark. I double up, thinking I am hearing policemen or overgrown schoolchildren running amuck at recess, throwing their arms like darts, swords. I waver inside of her voice and inside of her name. My head throbs. I cannot tell whether the phone has stopped ringing or not; at some point I think I hear a ring louder than all other rings, and a voice, not Maggie's voice, but another voice, a woman's voice, a slow Scottish accent, asking and begging for Crilly. But I am not sure.

I fall through shades of black and red and wonder if I am dreaming. Will you wait, Maggie? Will you call at the house? Will I see your slight and shaking form, your eyes shifty and sickly from an unwitting detox, your small quivering head, your rag-and-bone nails and skinny hand of screaming white? Don't ring, Maggie. Don't speak to my machine. I see you now on the Prince of Wales Road. You're walking my way with a dealer named Sport. You are sheathed in black cloth and your freckles are pale and many. You are still now, but a fence of tatty barbed wire courts and crevices behind you, stretching itself like a waking snake, miles and miles it is, bending and bent. Where are you going to, Maggie Delaney? Have you come for my man? Have you come for his drugs? Have you come to scorn me, to poke holes in my skin with those rag-and-bone nails, or to console me, saying, Claudia, I know you, you are just as I am, you are a lonely dandelion, as I am. A wily waif, a fallen wire, a forgotten fraud, a hoper of dope, a sick one, a sick one, body full of mucous, skin a-shining with seasonal sweat, legs heavy and still, eyes shutshutshut upon the brink of twilight, that horrible hour neither day nor night, horrible hour whatever will happen, horrible hour don't set your shoes upon that chalky broken pavement, don't dare set foot on that broken pavement, or you will die, yes die, stay put, stay put, your eyes shut, eyes shut, your head still, hot and still, try not to shake though your hands are quaking, try not to stir though your feet are sweating, try not to wake though your chest is heaving, please O please God try not to wake . . .

The telephone rings, is ringing now, and my lids flutter before my face. I answer.

'Yes?'

'Is that Claudia speakin'?' It is not Maggie. The Scottish one it is, the one with the begging voice.

'Yes.'

'This is Stella, here. You don't know me. I'm sure you've heard Crilly mention my name.'

I have. She used to be Crilly's stealing partner. She hit Boots, and Marks and Spencer while he had the bag. She is the crafty one. The one who never gets caught.

'Oh, yes.'

'Can you tell me where I can find him?'

'He's gone away for a while.'

'For how long, exactly?'

'I don't know.'

'The pigs have got him, haven't they?'

'I can't talk to you now, Stella. Please phone back another time.' I hang up. I have not met Stella, but I have seen her; a scrawny, gap-toothed, underfed Scot. In love with Crilly, or so I hear. She has an Iranian husband who is doing time, and two children in juvenile custody.

The heat of my room is stifling. I can't breathe. My bedroom flanks the street, it is on street level. I keep the windows shut, for fear of burglars and spiteful friends. I do not dare open the blinds. There are no tears but I make squeaky sounds with my mouth. In my groin there are twitchy, random jolts like the shorting of a fuse, as though a spatula has been thrust into me and wrapped around my uterus like a corkscrew. I lift myself, heaving to the bathroom, where the tile is cold and the eaves are cob-webbed. When I lower my head into that seatless bowl there is nothing, nothing. I run to my bed, recoiling. From outside, sounds grow louder; young ones shouting, oh godawful sounds — Jo, have you seen that cunt, he's shagging my bird . . . O stop please stop and I cover my ears. I must find Maggie.

Maggie has no phone, but I know where she works. It's night, it must be night now. I bathe and dress, and paste my face in gauzy liquid, whiting out the spots and the sweat. I drive to Highbury. The Oedipus Bull is a brightly lit pub full of architects and actors, loose linen trousers and girlfriends in off-the-shoulder black jerseys, tight around the bosom, their ears ablaze with silver and hoops, their hair short and bleached, '20s-style envelope-handbags, pencil ties . . . I half expect to see Gemma and her friends. I wouldn't mind, actually. I wouldn't mind seeing a familiar face or two.

I am waiting for Maggie to notice me. I wonder how they all can look so well. If they look well, then, are they well? Will I ever be well? Will the knot and sloth of me ever go away, leaving my body like a bad and finished dream? Maggie sails back and forth behind the counter, wearing a mini-dress, black tights, black pumps. She looks beautiful; almost placid. Upon closer inspection, only her eyes give her away, quick with the flicker of paranoia, scanning the room like marbles. She's looking for Crilly, for news. When she catches sight of me she smiles and I feel guilty for scorning her. We agree to talk once the last bell has rung. I sit for an hour, alone at a table with only one drink of scathing hard whiskey, which does not fall lightly upon my throat, but burns my mouth and neck with the sting of memory. Dave Brubeck is playing on the jukebox. I must be okay, I think. I have called to this pub to see a friend, the tall attractive barmaid in black, the Irish one, my lover's ex, by the way. Jazz is good. I don't look so bad. I'm drinking in Islington, calm as you like, why not?

The doors shut at last and Maggie comes with me to my car.
We sit without moving, gazing out at Upper Street.

'He's in prison, isn't he?' she asks.

'He will be.'

'I saw Stella. She told me.'

'How did she know?'

'Oh, she just knew.'

The sickness returns at the sound of strange names. I clutch
myself above the steering-wheel. The night is cold.

'Are you all right?' asks Maggie.

'I don't know. I think I need something.'

Maggie looks at me strangely. 'You're not addicted, are you?'
she asks. She's amused. I force a laugh. 'No, I'm upset. Do you
know where we can get a fix?'

Maggie pauses. 'Drive to Annie's house,' she says presently,
'in Camden Road.'

I do as I am told, though I don't know who Annie is. Maggie
tells me to wait in the car. I wait for fifteen minutes. Maggie
emerges slow and defeated. I recognise the posture; it is akin to
Crilly's, when his luck runs out.

'No joy.' We sit silently, the two of us, on the verge of tears. 'Is
there anywhere else we can go?' I ask.

'Not tonight. Annie and Chuck were having a huge row.
They're breaking up. They weren't too helpful.'

We settle for a bottle of Retsina; nasty cheap wine from the
local Greek's. At the Aegean Sea drunken middle-aged men
drink and sing and sputter as packs of walruses do, calling to us in
obscene and gravelly voices.

I switch the cocktail-glass on, the pink neon. I put on a
flamenco record and roll a joint. I'm not very good at it. The
process is painstaking. The answerphone flickers red from the
centre of the carpet; hesitantly I push the button. A message
from Gemma, concerned. And Stella, the begging Scot.

'How do you know Stella?' I ask Maggie.

Maggie opens the Retsina and takes off her jumper. Her shoulder-blades make sharp ripples in her skin. She's thin and bare.

'I've seen her around,' she says. 'The silly cow. She's always trying to tell me things.'

'What sort of things?'

'You know, don't you? You know what that ugly Jock's been saying about Crilly?'

'No, I don't know.'

'Well, then I don't know if I should tell you.'

I twitch. I try to be comfortable; to stretch my legs and think soothing thoughts. This is my home. This is my cushion. My sweet Spanish record.

'Go on, Maggie, you can't just start something and not finish it.'

Maggie pops the cork and pours cheerfully into water glasses. She is taking her time. I sip the wine. It is ghastly.

'Well, if you must know, she told us that she was leaving her husband, that scum-thief husband, and running away with Crilly. She said she was pregnant with his baby. I'm sure it was all her own pathetic fabrication. She heard you were pregnant and then told us that she was. She said to me once, "That stupid yank bitch, if it wasn't for her, I could have this baby".'

'So she had an abortion?'

'Well between you and me, she was never really pregnant. She just says things to get attention. She's a pathological liar. But you know, people talk. They know her; they don't really know you.'

'Who's "they"?'

'All the Camden lot. Annie. Chuck. Seamus and Marie and Perry . . .'

'But I know Seamus and Perry.'

'But you don't work with them. Stella's been working for Perry. She does all his dirty work for him. I'd say she's in love with him also. She spun a few yarns on that count, as well.'

'So Perry must know she's lying. About Crilly, I mean.'

'Yeah, I'd say Perry knows. But the others, I'm not sure. Stella will do anything for a man. She'll do the heavy stuff. Like when she stole with Crilly, she mostly took the risks while he just held the bag. They have to show their gratitude in some way.'

'But Crilly can't stand her, outside of work. He's always saying how she's so mad, so unattractive.'

'I know. I call her "Dirty Knickers".' Maggie leans back in the easy chair. I am amazed at her ease, why isn't she sick?

I move closer. I hang on her every word, the words and the way they are spoken.

'Maggie, you don't think . . .' I trail off. Maggie, who usually avoids eye contact for too long, keeps her face steady on mine.

'Claudia, I don't know. Probably not, but I simply don't know. There's something you have to understand about junkies. They're like cavemen. They don't trust anyone on the outside, anyone who appears to be on the outside. You're American. Your friends are straight. You have money, you like nice things. When a man as attractive as Crilly makes an attempt to leave the circle, the girls get bothered. Distressed. It's like they've lost a bodyguard.'

I close my eyes and swallow a gulp of Retsina.

'Crilly's a strange one,' she continues. 'Annie's been chatting to him quite a lot, lately. She says they've become close. He tells her all sorts of things.'

'What do you mean, "close"?'

'Oh, you know, good friends. I've a feeling that's why she was fighting with Chuck. No, I don't think he's fucking Dirty Knickers. But Annie, well, she's the sort that Crilly might find quite attractive.'

'But he's always with me, Maggie. We're together every single night and most of the day.'

'But that's not always, is it?'

'But he gave me such a hard time when I was unfaithful.'

'I know, fidelity means a lot to him. When we were together, he used to talk about it too. Maybe he's getting back at you. I remember when you were unfaithful. Several times. He told me about it.'

'He told you?'

'Remember, we're still pretty close.'

'Are you sleeping with Crilly, Maggie?'

'Me? God no. I've learned my lesson.'

'What lesson?'

'We had a fuck of a time. Towards the end, he slept with other women.'

'Do you know this for certain?'

'I think I do.'

'Well, what about you? Did you both mess around at the end?'

'Well, it's really very complicated. I'd rather not get into it.'

I wish to God I could vomit. But I've eaten nothing. I've taken nothing strong. I've only got heartburn. And Maggie has not finished talking.

'I'm only telling you these things because I like you, Claudia. I know you mean a lot to Crilly. But I wouldn't trust him. Not after the things that Annie was saying.'

'Is that why you went into Annie's alone?'

'No. I went in alone because they don't know you. If they had had gear, they wouldn't have served a stranger.'

'They know who I am.'

'Barely. They think they know.'

'What do you mean?'

'They don't really know what to make of you. Annie thinks that you're not worth worrying about. That you're temporary.'

'Didn't you correct them, Maggie? Didn't you see them straight?'

'No, it wasn't worth it. I didn't want to make any trouble.'

'What trouble?'

'I told you. They're vicious. They're like a tribe. Anyone outside their immediate circle is suspect.'

'Are you one of them?'

'God no. I've broken away from that whole junkie crowd. I'm doing that computer course in the spring. Some of the women resent me for it. And they resent Crilly for living with you. I know you're good for him. I've told him so.'

I decide not to speak. I give her the chance to redeem herself. She doesn't. It's late. I give Maggie sheets and a duvet. Of course I cannot sleep, and my body is feverish with tremors and the shrieking of women's names. At four a.m., just when I've drifted beneath the surface layer, the telephone rings. I jolt upright.

'Claudia, it's Stella, here.'

'What do you want?'

'I'm sorry to bother you, Claudia. I'm not your enemy. I just want to know where Crilly is.'

'Your guess is as good as mine.'

'Ah, come on, Hen. You can tell me. Brixton?'

'No.'

'Pentonville. They've sent him to Pentonville, esn't tha' right?'

'Leave me alone, Stella.'

'I just want to see him. The poor lad must be dyin'.'

'So?'

'So you can tell where he is and I'll bring him something nice. We don't want him to be sick now.'

'Stella, leave him be. He'll get clean and start a new life.'

'I completely agree. But it's early now, early detox is dangerous . . . think of Crilly now, think of Crilly.'

'I can't seem to stop thinking about him.'

'If I know Crilly, he'll be dyin' . . .'

I hang up the phone. I hold my shivering knees and stare at the shadows on the walls.

In the morning, Maggie proposes that we smuggle some gear to Crilly. She tells me it's dangerous to let him go without. She tells me his habit is bigger than I know, that at other people's homes, he shoots dope into his arm. My head congests. Thankfully, she leaves.

On the third day, I am strong enough to wash and do my laundry. I sit down at my desk and write a letter of accusations to Crilly. I sleep easily, rising before ten the following morning, to post my letter. I shop. I buy a new dress. In the evening, I meet friends at the Devonshire for a drink. I say that I have been sick with flu. They believe me. I attend college for the first time in weeks. Much to my amazement the tutors don't yell. On Friday, I receive a letter.

Jezebel . . .

Don't listen to a word they say. They are scumbags.

All I think about is you.

At night, I hold my excuse for a pillow,

and think about your face and your hair and your

incredible eyes. I never look at another. FOR THE LOVE

OF ME AND OF US MY GOD DON'T LISTEN! I'm

clean as a whistle and soon I'm coming home to you. My

cellmate's from Liverpool. I want you to meet him. Maybe

we can go to Liverpool. We'll go to Glasgow. We'll go to

Dublin. Anything to get away. I'm clean, my love, I'm

gonna make a go of it. I love you more than me own self.

On me mother's life. We'll go away from them all I can't

wait to see you . . .

In the evening, I call into the Oedipus Bull. I walk straight over to Maggie.

'Why did you lie to me?' I ask her.

'What do you mean?'

'You know he hasn't been unfaithful.'

'Well, I could have made a mistake.'

'You lied.'

Maggie shrugs, unperturbed. 'Who knows who's lying? I was only trying to give you some support, Claudia.'

'Keep it.'

I go to court on the day that Crilly is released. He looks wonderful; prison has fattened him and his cheeks are pink and shiny, as though he has been working out of doors. He looks like a Viking. We stroll arm in arm to the nearest pub and I buy him a freedom drink and lunch; a pint of stout and a Ploughman's. It is as though he's been inside for months. He tells me about the men he met in prison, imitating their varied dialects with great skill.

'I'm gonna do it this time, Claudia,' he says, his mouth full of stout and his arm about my shoulder. 'I'm gonna stay clean. I don't need those pratts. I may even get a job.'

Yet when we return home, the flat feels strange; too tidy, almost barren. I expect Crilly to ravish me, as promised by letters scrawled in lustful, sweeping biro, but he doesn't. The phone rings. It is Maggie for Crilly. While he speaks to her I leave the room, slamming the door behind me. Presently Crilly joins me. He holds me close.

'She invited us both down for a drink.'

'You go.'

'She invited us both down.'

'You go.' We lie in silence.

'I won't go,' he says after a minute. 'We won't go.'

Newly clean, freshly washed, appetites intact, eyes alert, we are here now, together. And we can't think of one fucking thing to do. We decide to see a film. We take the car.

'Feels grand to be in the old heap again,' says Crilly. I smile at him. We drive silently down Kentish Town Road. Crilly's eyes widen at his surroundings: the post office, Woolworth's, Perfect Pizza, Salter Rex Estate Agents, dogs, fruit markets. They make him anxious. When we reach the fork at Royal College Street, Crilly points to a block of flats.

'That's where the McKloskey brothers are livin'. Maggie says they're servin'.'

I don't reply.

'She says it's a quick operation,' he continues.

'Rubbish. It's never quick. It'd take ages.'

'That's not true,' he speaks softly. 'Surely your memory isn't so short. Sometimes it's quicker than buyin' a pack of fags in the pub.'

I stop the car. We sit staring ahead. When I turn to him, his face is streaked with tears.

'I want to make love to you, Claudia,' he says, 'I want to hold you in my arms all night tru', I want to tell you what it's been like for me without you, just missing you, missing you so bad like one of us had passed on. I want to be with you, really with you, inside you for hours on end, I'm achin' for it.'

I take his hand. 'You can,' I say. 'You *can*.'

Crilly kisses my hand and holds it against his mouth. His tears are hot to the touch.

'No,' he says, straining, 'I don't know how.'

I take him in my arms and hold him. When I try to move back, he clings.

I pull away.

'Can't we just try, Crilly?' I plead, as I am also pleading to myself. 'Like we said before, all those things we said before?'

Crilly thinks for a moment. He gazes off to one side.

'I look at your face, and I look at one eye and then the other and then your nose, but I can't seem to look at your face altogether, all at once, because the sight of your face is causing me pain.'

He is right, this time. He isn't long.

The light is dim and pink. We make love until our flesh melts about our thighs, our genitals, the sore bits. We gaze at one another despite the effort of heavy lids, our nodding heads, until the lull of sleep defeats. We have, we have, we have, the finest time.

Yet when I awake to the next day and my leaden legs, the flat is dark with disrepair — the light in the fridge has gone out, the milk is off. I crawl like a rat to that methadone clinic, re-enlist for Kathleen McGuire, the prettier one, the easy one. I get a note to customs, signed by Geraldine. I stop at the chemist for that great big bottle, gangbusters green, my ticket home. While Crilly sleeps, there are calls, arrangements, the sound of my own soapy voice, a sallow sound, a sweaty sound. As the shallow tent of evening falls upon us, and black taxis queue like hearses at Marble Arch, I lift my knees to the platform, glide down the Westway with my head full of phlegm and board that plane to Los Angeles. I am flying now, flying home through that murky sky which is neither here nor there, neither day nor night, and in the sponge of my saturated soul, I feel so very little.

reunion

I cower from Los Angeles, so vast and bright, exposed in pink and green, a sickly sprawl. I avoid my family and hover low in bed beneath their footsteps, avoiding their questions and their kitchen smells — basil and sage and *crème anglaise*. I will annihilate everything. All smells, all chatter. All that has been done and mostly the waste of all that I have never done. It is the holiday season. I have left London. I have left Crilly. My future is bottled in an emerald flask in the bottom drawer, hidden in my passport and a sombre seven pound twenty of English money.

I am scheduled to visit a reunion of old friends. High school friends. Some I have seen in recent years, most I have not. I dread the occasion, but I have no choice, somehow.

It's a link to sanity, I tell myself. To school. My last link, maybe.

Rhianon calls for me at my house. Rhianon is a dancer and she lives in a Buddhist retreat in Maine. She has great blue eyes and wispy grain-coloured hair and though she is muscular, her features have a look of fragility to them, freckled and flushed. In school, we were close. Rhianon is an excellent listener, a mistress of empathy. She wears Indian clothing and patchouli oil, is given to claustrophobia in the city, and mourns the death of her sister as though it were yesterday.

When I answer the door, she is ashen. She searches my face for something familiar. I try to make her laugh, to put energy into my words, to make sense, but I know it is futile. Before I have spoken or embraced her even, I have betrayed her. This makes me angry.

'When I look at you,' she admits in the car, 'I get dizzy. Your eyes are swimming. What have you done to yourself?'

'I'm on my last legs of this thing,' I say, 'and I have a terminal case of jet lag. It's been a rough year. I had hoped you wouldn't notice.'

We discuss former classmates. Rhianon poses lively curiosities over who is doing what and living where. I writhe in contempt for the whole lot of them. This one is pristine, that one is pretty, another is banal and stupid and shallow. I long for the evening and the end, when Rhianon and I can return home and drink tea and watch a video. But Rhianon is annoyed.

'I don't want to be sandwiched between their lives and your hatred,' she says. 'Perhaps it's okay for you to feel this way now; or maybe you're even right about the things you say. But I don't want to feel the way you're feeling, and your venom is contagious.'

I have never heard Rhianon use this tone before. I feel condemned.

'I know that you're right,' I say, 'but I can't help it. I hate this "unity" crap, it's just so contrived. What have we all got in common anyway? I can't identify with anybody these days. I hate America; all these mini-malls and bright streets. Sometimes I wish I could just stick my finger down my throat and puke up my whole ugly past and the country along with it.'

Rhianon drives slowly; the wheels of her car run jagged and upset.

'I've missed you,' she says.

We go on in silence.

Everyone looks splendid, with the exception of myself. Helen bustles forward to greet us; she wears white from head to toe and her hair is loose and flowing and blonde, her face empty of make-up, unflawed and phosphorous. We were close in school; I adored her family, their fragrant, forested hideaway in Nicholas Canyon, their photos and cushions and hostess treats for after school and Cokes only on weekends. Once, I caught flu when Mom and Larry were out of town, and Charlotte, Helen's mother (who bore an incredible resemblance to Helen) took me in and set me up in Helen's bed beneath the lace canopy, and served me cinnamon toast and hot chocolate. She would not let me watch television but read to me instead from a volume of nursery rhymes and the tales of Grimm. Though I was thirteen, I felt suddenly six, finally six. I have not seen Helen's family in eight years. This shames me. I avoid thinking of them. Helen became an anchorwoman. She married and bought a house in Los Feliz. As she greets us, her voice is high and happy and frenetic, and she speaks quickly, telling us things, asking us things. I stand and try to listen, to ignore the strangle of insects in my head, pressing against my bladder, the something-left-of-innards crushed and tumbled in my belly, the chooka-churning gotta gotta gotta gotta . . . groping like rush hour, patterned as a freeway pile-up. As though my hearing is impaired, I only catch slivers of conversation, of information; Rhianon's new dance company, Helen's network, houses, food, wonderful concerts, exciting people, great, if kind of weird, to have us all here again.

I am teeming, bashing, full of hate.

I back away and wander through the crowd. It is not so many familiar faces that I see, but the distortion of them, faces as they see me, quizzical, anxious, opaque. I must be imagining their disdain; projecting my poison onto unwitting people, as Rhianon said.

I see myself at sixteen with a car full of people, my memory scented with clove cigarettes and French toast from Dupars. I'm speeding down the highway, The Clash on my car stereo, chatter at the prospect of something new, a new lover, a new film, a new thing to do on a Saturday night. The vision is vivid; it stings. I go to the toilet and slosh myself with water and stare at my anaemic face, my hair as limp as beans, hair that has lost its curl to the oppressive flatness of beds, hair greasy though I have only just washed it. I force myself to emerge.

Anne is an intellectual, a shining alumnae in slim-waisted trousers and a tuxedo shirt. She is directing a film for some Swedish guy worth knowing. She looks as she has always looked; boyish, clean, immaculate.

I tell her I am working as a barmaid. I say I have no other aspirations. I tell her that as soon as I can, I will move to Northumberland and work at a Northumberland pub. Then I will move to Yorkshire and work at a pub there. I will spend my entire life working at pubs. There is much to learn behind the bar. Much to see.

They are lies, all of them. Lies as true as anything I could say.

A former classmate called Leticia, whom I have never known well, drinks citrus nectar by the fruit bar. She is a starlet. Men and women mill about her, or glance discreetly at her from a distance. She has a mane of black hair and sultry eyes and she wears a simple dress, silk ochre. As I pass I hear her saying, 'Every film I'm in I get raped; I don't know whether I'm typecast or what.'

But she seems happy. Serene. Successful in life and in loin.

'Are you seeing anybody?' asks Tom Finkelstein, a lawyer. I jerk my head; I realise he is talking to me. When did we begin talking? My God was I nodding, was I goofing off, where were my eyes just then, didn't I belch just now and fill my mouth with the cough mixture taste of methadone, that sweet friendly surge of mine? I don't remember when we started talking.

Am I seeing anybody?

Oh yes, of course. My love is pure and methodical like a circle.

He is as healthy as oats when he is inside of me.

You're a sorry slug, I want to say to Tom Finkelstein. You're a pathetic monk. A mindless moron, a squawker, a thief of life, a robber of fate. You know nothing. Fuck all about anything. Nothing. Never a love could be unrequited as mine. Never, and never.

But then, I don't really know Tom Finkelstein, not well enough to hate him, anyway.

I back away; Tom's face is lined as though I have insulted him aloud. I know that I have insulted him, silently somehow, or maybe with words, but I can't remember what's been said, though I only said it seconds ago.

I try to eat and nearly gag. The buffet is long and salubrious, ablaze with tails of things and heads of things and fruity stuff of some obscene orange.

Across the room, Stephanie sits with her hair loping about her face. I make my way to her. Stephanie and I have always shared a love of words and reviews and assessments. As early as eleven, there were books to be discussed, people to be evaluated, films to be conquered. I approach her. She looks up briefly but does not acknowledge me; nor does she stop talking. She is telling Rhianon about her Icelandic Legends course. Rhianon's eyes stray sheepishly to mine.

'Are you all right, Claudia?' she asks, at the nearest pause.

'I'm trying.' I can feel without touching it the beginnings of a rash on my face; some sort of heat rash, though it is not hot.

I ask Stephanie how long she's been in town. Stephanie replies that she has been in L.A. for two weeks. Her tone is so flat I hardly recognise it. She does not lift her head to look up at me.

'I didn't know. Why haven't you phoned?'

Stephanie has an overwhelming heap of hair. She plays with it.

'I didn't think it was a good idea.'

Rhianon smiles at me, touches my shoulder, edges away.

'Why not?' I sit in Rhianon's place.

'It just didn't seem the wise thing to do.'

I pursue it, though I know I shouldn't. Eventually she meets my eyes.

'We shouldn't be friends, Claudia. Our versions of reality are just too different.'

'What the hell does that mean?'

'I don't think we should get into this here.'

'Then where will we get into it? At the lunch we won't have after you haven't phoned me?'

'It's a reunion.'

'Listen, the least you can do is explain.'

Stephanie pauses. 'Okay,' she says finally, 'I'll level with you. I don't feel that you're honest about your life. The way you present yourself is light years from the way you really are.'

'Just say what you mean, Stephanie.'

'Fine. Your world is steeped in fantasy. Even in high school you used to spend years bereaving affairs you'd never even had. And yet you expected everyone else to be an accomplice to your fantasies, to your delusions. And we bought it because you were so persuasive.'

'This is about high school?'

'No. It's about always. It was the fantasies you created for yourself, that you expected us all to take part in. All that Lady of the Mansion shit. Treating people as pawns, as characters in some ludicrous play of yours. But that's only part of it. An example, if you will. There's more to it than that. You're such a slave to your emotions that you forget common courtesy and consideration. You'll obsess or break down over a trifle, but when terrible things happen to you, or you do terrible things, you don't seem to mind or even notice. Someone who lets herself get five months pregnant without realising it is not a healthy person. A heroin addict is not a healthy person —'

'What makes you say that, who told you that?' I swallow myself, I interrupt.

Stephanie stares at me for a moment. Go on, I'm thinking, say the rest, tell me I'm a liar and a junkie and a liability, a thief and a scumbag, a slut. Tell me please, I want you to. Tell me.

But she just stares.

'You're silly, Claudia,' she says at last. 'You're just so awfully silly.'

Stephanie gathers herself and walks away. I sit slumped with my head in my hands. When I look up, crowds of people are milling about one another like s-shapes, and the smell of dry-cleaning sticks in my nostrils, along with the floral of expensive cologne and the musk of fermenting fruit. It rots and swells like a tornado within me. I would like to be an ocean, the Pacific Ocean off Long Beach, murky and toxic from an oil spill. I would flood that stretch of weedy sand just south of the Santa Monica pier, and I will rape and violate that sand, for all its seaweed and dead baby crabs and empty Coors and Michelob beer cans, and I will strike clear up against the public ladies' restroom wall — reeking as it does of salt and shit and urine — and THRASH like a bastard till the wave is knocked out of me and I am left with nothing but a defeated pool of polluted water. And I am powerless to drain from the tenement hell of public restrooms, and I am too benign to lick torrid obscenities from the chipped and concrete wall . . .!

At four a.m., I lie feverish with familiar faces crumbling before me as though they were paper burning through with fire from the edges to their centres. My body is so drenched that I can hardly lift it; I wonder at one point whether I have fallen into a coma, simply forgetting how to move. The methadone isn't working. I pick up the phone and phone London. Crilly answers, his voice heavy. But I can hear his chest lift at the sound of my weeping.

All these words, so many words, tumble out, babble horribly. Crilly won't you come and stay with me, won't you, won't you. I can't stand it, I have no one but you, please come and be with me . . .

You know I can't, he says, you know I can't, there is no money, the pigs have my passport, I can't my baby Jezebel, why did you ever leave me?

But why can't you? Fuck the rest, the reasons. Fuck it all. Come be with me and nurse my body and squeeze me tight inside of yourself.

Crilly's crying, O he's crying now, the Mick, the bastard, O be strong for a while why don't you, be strong for me, they say I'm a liar and a junkie. They hate me, and I need you on my chest and in my breath and hovering close in my single bed.

They're jealous, he says, and means it too.

No, I tell him, they're right. O Crilly, let's move to Scotland, you and I. You can get a job as a shepherd and I'll be a shepherdess. No one will know us and they'll all love us. I know a place in the Highlands where we can buy a croft for five grand. Or we'll move to the Outer Hebrides and learn to speak Gaelic. We'll sing folk songs in the local pub. We'll herd sheep. I'll learn to love those sheep. We'll get hundreds of cats and one of those collie sheepdogs. We'll train the sheepdog to love the cats. You'll be a shepherd and I'll be a shepherdess. Can we do it? Will you think about it?

His sounds are low and muffled, gasping like I've cut his throat.

Claudia — he says my name so low that I can hardly hear him — I wish I could touch you.

'Can we Crilly?'

His breathes his pause, sticks in me throat, that sobbing again.

When he does speak I notice the slur and the languid tone, the drip of smack and sulphur in his voice.

'Please . . . try and get some sleep, my girl,' he says, in the voice that never sleeps, that has never slept, that is dying to just be dying. I hang up the phone and lie back on my pillow, thinking strangely of words and what they mean. Love. Luv. Luv's Baby. Soft Diapers. Sheep. Sheepish. Cry. Cri. Crilly. 'Elite' is a brand of cheap nail polish. 'Lorry' is a truck. 'Smack' is a hit, a strike, a punch. 'Work' is something that grown-ups do. 'Works' are something you keep in the kitchen drawer, behind the plastic bags . . . I think of nothing but words, names, colours. By dawn, sleep descends upon me and kisses me gently, quenching the vacant valley, sleepless fear, furious fate, fever, famine. I fall deep asleep, asleepy, asleeping. All is forgiven.

the last supper

By the 31st of December, I have 30ml of methadone left, diluted with water in a tragic attempt to prolong it. It will barely last me two days, without much of a high. There is a New Year's party somewhere, but I can't remember whose it is, where it is. I am sick with myself for rationing the stuff so poorly, for taking indulgent gulps whenever the slightest fatigue takes me, whenever my nerves threaten to scatter and rise. I think of my methadone counsellor, lovely Geraldine, stern and concerned in pleated skirts and glasses, posing gentle questions, sitting cross-legged against the tattered walls of her cubicle. I think of the clinic itself; the reception, dusty windows through which peep only the most hesitant shades of day, and the restless, broken-skinned patients bundled in cheap cardigans, dragging carrier bags of Four X lager and dull-faced babies in plastic prams.

In the elegant Spanish brightness of my mother's house, I feast on the image of the clinic, such a tawdry place in winter, and of Geraldine, as I stand before the mirror with my meek and futile 30ml. It was bleak, the clinic. But a comfort to me just the same.

I miss those faces now, those weary everyday sighs, the slow advice, the tatty steel desks and second class stamps and the old lady at the chemist taking my prescription to be filled, daily. 'You going on holiday?' she asked on the very last day, glancing at Geraldine's letter, a rare request for quantity, and then bagging the bottle.

'I'm going home to California.'

'I wish I was going there. Me 'usband won't even go to Blackpool for the holidays.'

'That's a pity.'

'I'll live. I have to work, anyway. You're from entertainment people, 'nt ya?'

'I suppose I am.'

'Your boyfriend told me when he come in for 'is medication. 'e's a fine bloke, for an Irishman. Handsome, too.'

'Yes, he is.'

'I used to be in entertainment. I used to sing live at pubs in Stepney. You ever been to the Cheater's Head?'

'I can't say that I have.'

'Or the Bull and Milkmaid? The women's face was drawn in fine, long lines tugging at the corners of her mouth.

'I'm afraid not. Not yet, anyway.'

'We 'ad a ferocious crowd in there. Then again, that was thirty, forty years ago. Can't say what it's like now. Probably just the jukebox. They all listen to that Kylie Minogue dribble, don't they?'

'I'm afraid so.'

'I can't stand the sight of her. Mind you, she's got a good figure.'

'I'd rather listen to you.'

'Bless you, darlin'. Happy Christmas. And the next time you come in, you'll be past all this, just stoppin' in to buy shampoo or a pair of them earrings, two for a fiver.'

'Yes, maybe.'

'You're a nice girl.'

This was the last thing she said.

·

'Junkie,' I shout to myself in the mirror, and then I giggle, feeling like an infant who has sworn and recognises the bite of the word 'fuck' on her lips. I am tired. The thought of the New Year is deafening, disgusting even. The sparkling journal I bought at Alexander's Stationers, so steadily lined, brazen with resolutions, slit me a paper cut on the side of a page. I almost cut all my hair off after that. Almost dunked my face in the toilet. But I daren't be so dramatic. I don't dare to live this day. I don't dare to walk and talk and drive, as though I could do like the others do, as though I was a normal person who does her laundry and changes lightbulbs and washes the sink from time to time. I know, as he knows, there is only one thing I have to look forward to.

(And maybe a thing or two from before — my mother in her peach halter, her back slender and white, her high giggle, the giggle of delight and fresh sloping green hills . . . And Daddy, those Sunday smells, my name spelt with pancake batter on the griddle, those Norman Rockwell smells.)

I'm back to syrup now. That's what I look forward to each day for as long as I dare to hold out, for every quivering moment that dares to precede it, each and every day that syrupy dollop feels real to me, evades the fear of daylight and the forms milling about my mother's house or wily strangers at the 7–11 on Franklin buying beers and Bigwheels.

When I first arrived, a week or so ago, I tried to go without it, and I lunched at Muse with my mother. I broke into a sweat by the time the prawns in sauce arrived. The walls went seasick and diagonal, some kind of spiralling orange like a Dali painting. I clenched myself against the ludicrous contrast of those cool, white, skylit surfaces, of pretty waiters sailing back and forth like easy boats. I told my mother I had jet lag. I could not even drink a glass of white wine. After lunch, we stopped to rent a car for me. Mom stood at the desk and filled out the paperwork, while I doubled over on the grey-flecked terrycloth, fake wood panelling on either side of me, the smell of ammonia and pine air freshener thick in my face and mouth and stomach. When I returned home I took 25ml (10ml more than I was supposed to), slept for a little while, and rose cheerfully. The muscle of sickness subsided into languidness again and I was fit to make plans for the evening, and to see old friends whose names had so shocked with the terror of familiarity only an hour or so before.

I have no life without it. Without it, there is only sickness, paranoia, paralysis. And hate. I hate everybody: Larry and my mother as they squabble over the entertainment section of the *New York Times*; my brother who talks every moment he is awake and eats horrendous portions of food at every meal and fidgets in the face of silence; I hate doorbells and telephones and supermarkets and the hard clench the emergency brake makes when you put the car in park.

In the mirror, I am a mess of sticky white, whiter than the English, shapeless as a pillow, tired, very tired. There are American friends to face, those remaining. I hate them because they can hear me and they can see me. And what is worse, I hate them for their honest livings, their jaunts to the gym, for the scripts they are writing or acting classes they are attending or answerphone messages they are leaving for one another. I hate their salads, their cars, their clothes, their bodies. At least in London, we had humility; we ground closely together, we ate cheap curries once the pubs shut, our skin chipped with the cold in winter. We laughed at everyone, we laughed at ourselves. I am ugly now. I am heathen. I have nothing to offer but a broken body, a quivering skin, a mind stuffed with words, but no history, no befores.

New Year's Eve. Alone in the house of my family while they ski in Colorado. My hands are damp. I want my lover on a summer afternoon on the hilly stretch of grass before the museum in Hampstead Heath, rolling fat joints for us, laced with heroin. I want my mother with her jet black hair loose and long, rolling down that hill, snuggling me to a bicycle seat and me as tiny and snug as a baby chick. And the touch of a silver tube pressed to my princess lips. I could die in front of this very mirror, sank down to the carpet, just simply and happily die. But thinking is such a busy thing.

I used to tell long and animated stories.

I used to make people laugh.

I used to be less afraid of people, or was I?

I used to be pretty.

Tomorrow is 1990. And another crampy and perspiring winter, too weak to get out of bed while the sun still shines, munching on small paper bags of white chocolate mouse figurines from Woolworth's in the Kentish Town Road. And that dank underground where the escalator never runs. Down the spiral of steps with the piss puddles and the old, barren scouse woman, huddled among thin blankets and carrier bags.

'Have you got 50p for me and my man?'

Me and my man. The sweet relief of scoring quickly, a £20 bag cut without too much sugar. If the nights could go on forever, with my eyes a-swimming and my deft fingers scratching the sweet itch of stoned skin, with no stark ugly mornings in store to mock us, no shrill cries of the telephone, no sunshine in our wake to embarrass us, then we would live, Crilly and I, peaceful in our reverie, like saints in Heaven. We'd light candles for our souls. I would never venture near bright light nor explain myself to inquiring faces. Crilly and I would occupy one single spot beneath the lavender neon, and it would be a static, unconditional, eternal place. A place of rest without daily living, without body temperature, without sickness or money or remorse.

I am suddenly ravenous for ritual. A divorce. A wake. A

prayer. If only I knew how to pray, I would. Instead, I appeal to the mirror.

If I go to the party, I will die.

If I stay at home, I will surely die.

At the stroke of midnight, I will die.

I fall to my knees.

Don't let me die.

I cry a little, in a tearless way, wondering where the water has gone.

Abandon me, my opiate saint, to the New Year, solemn and sick as it may be.

No more.

I take the methadone from the drawer and swallow the lot. There is nothing left. Nothing left to survive the eve of '90. I'm on my squeaky knees now. There is no turning back.

In the days that follow, I postpone withdrawal, plying myself with librium and valium from Larry's medicine chest. The weight of my body is so oppressive that I sleep for five days.

On the fifth day, my mother and Larry and Polly return from Colorado. It is Winchell's twelfth birthday. I am expected to attend his party, which is to be held at a '50s diner. Twelve twelve-year-olds are invited. But I'm not moving from this bed.

'What's wrong with you?' my mother asks, her long face flushed with ski-burn.

'I don't know.' Aware of my slurring words, I try to push them out properly. 'I'm tired.'

'Are you sick?'

'I don't know.'

Larry comes to the doorway. 'What is it?' he asks, his features quick and gaunt, his posture clenched and angry. 'Do you have flu?'

'Maybe.'

'Do you have a temperature?'

My mother feels my forehead. 'You don't have fever.'

I fall back down to the pillow. My mother's voice rises.

'You're supposed to help with the party. You're supposed to drive,' she says. Her urgency annoys me. I turn on my side.

'You have 35 dollars worth of overdue videos.'

'I'll pay for them.'

'That's not the point. How can you just let it go like that?'

My eyes close. I see an Irish field. When was the potato famine: now? a hundred years ago? Once, while at the pub with Scottish Billy McGregor, we met an American called Cliff who thought that Ireland and Scotland were the same. He asked Billy, 'You guys still have a potato problem up there or what?' He was a fool, Chicago Cliff. He was the same guy who said, 'What you say we get a whole van of people together and go to Dover for the day? I hear they have pretty good seafood up there.' Dover! Honestly!

'Claudia!'

I start, and sit up.

'You have to get ready. Winchell's party is in an hour!'

'Why aren't you skiing?' I'm suddenly worried about this. I worry hard.

There is an audible pause from the doorway. It's terrible. I can feel them looking at one another, a grave glance, prolonged and obnoxious. My eyes water.

'Go, please, Larry,' I slur. 'I want to be alone with Mommy.'

After a moment's hesitation, Larry leaves. My mother stands still, silent with alarm.

'I'm very sick, Mommy. I think I might have AIDS.'

I instantly regret the lie, but I want her to stop talking about Winchell's party. I want her to understand without knowing anything. Presently, through a thick haze of sedative, I tell my mother the truth.

Dr Stephen Sullivan is a friend of the family; a good man with a wife and three sons, one Winchell's age. He has pale blond hair and a gently lined face and a square jaw. We spend our Christmas dinners with Stephen and his wife Jenny at their house in Los Feliz. Though Stephen is a dedicated doctor, he writes mystery stories in his spare time, and some have been published in a shiny volume by a small publishing house. Stephen loves England, he asks me about it. He is a fine audience for my sentimental ramblings, my Somersets, my Scotlands.

Still catatonic with downers, I allow my mother to take me to him. I have never seen his office, or him in his white doctor's coat. I sit in the sterile cubicle, aware of how heavy my lids are, how white and plain I am, and how unkempt, with my hair unbrushed for days and falling about my eyes as though it, too, were on downers. Just last week I sat at his table in my black silk dress and silver earrings, my eyes painted well and shiny, my neck perfumed. He has never seen my naked face. I avert my eyes. Stephen speaks softly, cautious not to offend. He asks what I have taken.

I tell him. 'I don't know how much. I'm so tired.' My voice is slow like crusted treacle . . .

'And before?'

I tell him. It's an incredible effort to remember.

'So you took the pills to calm you?'

I nod, mumbling, 'Is that bad?'

'No.' Stephen is still as he speaks to me. His brow is furrowed. His eyes do not leave my face.

'How much heroin were you taking generally, can you give me a rough idea?'

Again, this delicacy, and Christ I don't know. I tell him
so.

'It changed so much all the time.'

'But you were taking both methadone and heroin simul-
taneously.'

'Yeah, but I never shot it.' I push up my sleeve to show an
absence of track marks. My eyes well a little. He looks, he nods.
Was it this Christmas or the Christmas before, he was talking
about Cornwall? He wanted to rent a house and write there. He
knew an eccentric, a native Cornish man who spoke Cornish,
with whom he drank port and brandy. The man had the most
comprehensive set of antiquarian books he had ever seen. I
strain my memory. It bothers me that I can't remember whether
it was one week past or one year past. It bothers me a lot.

'I don't want to be sick,' I say.

'Well the thing is, it takes some time for methadone to leave
the body. Longer than heroin even.'

'Oh. Yes, I think that. My boyfriend told me.'

'Is he still using?'

'I don't know. I'm gonna be sick, I know it.' I challenge him to
free me. He explains that Clonidine will reduce my symptoms,
but a nasty withdrawal is inevitable no matter what I take. He
says he will give me something to help me sleep, but only for a
while.

I hold my face in my hands. I look up. He is standing there,
still.

'Stephen?'

'Yes.'

'Could you tell at Christmas? When I was all dressed up and
everything? Could you tell I was hooked?'

'Not exactly. I could see something wasn't quite right.'

I search his face for signs of judgement or condemnation.
There are none. His brow does not unwrinkle, he is perfectly

still, as though he knows that I might shatter at the slightest movement.

'I know how I must seem now,' I say helplessly.

'You've had a hard time of it, Claudia.'

I hold it back. I take a deep breath to speak.

'But what I don't understand is, why can't I just keep on? With the methadone, I mean? I mean, I take it and I feel fine . . . not stoned, but fine, just like me. I feel like me. I can talk to people and drive and go out of the house. It makes me feel . . . oh, just fine. Just like me. Why can't I keep on?'

Stephen pauses.

'Why can't I just go on?' I ask again.

'Well, you could,' he says after a moment, 'except that one day you'll wake up and you'll realise that it's not you. The same way that on some mornings, I . . . on some mornings, I . . . wake up and know that I don't really want to be a doctor.'

I think for a moment, and my mind snaps, becomes lucid almost. Of course, he wants to be a writer! I flash upon his family, his three sons who look exactly like him, his mystery stories. His friend in Cornwall with the antiquarian book collection. His Christmas dinners and his wife's lamb roast and his youngest son playing Nintendo on the video. And the bright volume of stories, distributed by a small London publishing House. Dr Stephen Sullivan wants to be a writer.

I put my hands in my face and I weep, for real this time.

detox

It is disheartening to apply a supposed panacea to myself through a round white patch stuck to the skin. This thing called Clonidine, usually given to heart patients, is meant to reduce the symptoms of early withdrawal, but it has no impact that I can feel. Junkie that I am, I have a distinct mistrust of anything that is not experienced immediately. I want to feel something always. I want to feel a great deal of something unreal, extreme or ecstatic. Heroin was wonderful until the euphoria left me; then it was numbing, then it was nothing. Now it is nothing, a painful nothing, just a violent wordiness in my head, palpitations in my heart. Or at least, I think it is my heart.

But I trust in Stephen Sullivan. I long to soothe the spasms of withdrawal, if only because Stephen wishes it for me, so I have faith in the sterile white patches. I have faith in the clean floral sheets that the Guatemalan housekeeper dresses my bed with. I even have faith in the Mormon pamphlets she leaves by my bedside. Well, not faith, exactly. I have not yet learned faith, but I realise that I have nothing to put in its stead, nothing better to offer. At least the crisp white of sheets and patches constitutes a sense of convalescence, of finishing, mending, dying. I accept the fact, if ungraciously, of my withdrawal now; shuddering and shaking in my skin, waiting to be well, waiting to be worse. If I could be bled by leeches, as sick people were in the Middle Ages, then I would. Anything to suck the poison away. But there is no sucking. Only time.

The first fortnight is the worst. I take religiously to my bed, and perspire heavily, unable to sleep. I feel as though I am in a state of perpetual epilepsy; my body twitching from somewhere deep and nameless within itself, my skin dry and papery as dying leaves, my eyes watering. Cramps throb in limbs I didn't know I had. I am sure I can feel the marrow in my bones, and that it is green as rancid yoghurt. I cannot eat. I leave the house only to see my therapist. As I am unable to drive, a taxi takes me there on my first day. The driver is a half-Mexican, half-Italian beer-gutted veteran who was in the army with Elvis. He gives me a joint and offers to buy me heroin without prompting from myself. This mystifies me, as for all the years I have lived in Los Angeles, I have never been offered heroin. And now! I take the joint but decline the heroin, feeling slight and noble. On the second day, my mother drives me. I slump in comatose fashion with my head leaning diagonally across the car headrest. My mother says I look as though I have been embalmed. The morning is sunny. There are many cars on Franklin. I despise every one of them. Mama complains about the traffic, and in my head I beg her to stop.

My therapist, Dr Jane Hanson, is an attractive woman in her mid-thirties who wears grey man-tailored suits that match the carpet. She works from a narrow office in west Los Angeles, with only one window facing a brick wall. On the second day, I tell her about the taxi driver. Her eyes are cool, wide and steady, a frigid blue. Her skin is very white. She asks if I am agitated, suicidal. I reply that yes, I am agitated but I could not be bothered to kill myself.

'You have no will,' she says to me.

'I suppose I haven't.'

'You know that the odds are stacked heavily against you.'

'I wasn't sure.'

'You should know. Very few heroin addicts recover.'

'You act as though you can't help me.'

'I don't know if I can.'

The tears come, as they always do; just another spasm. Jane offers me a tissue but remains aloof, very still, in her straight yellow chair that does not swivel. She leans in to me, her elbows on her knees. I look not at her but at her nylons, runless, seamless.

'Claudia,' she says, 'know that the odds are stacked against you. You have no morality, no bedrock. Your family has neglected you. You spent half your adolescence in the back room of your father's house, and the other half in the beds of strange men. Your parents are good people but they taught you no ethics, no discipline. You don't know how to love people or how to be loved. You have always been searching for a way out, an escape. Through drugs, through sex, through fantasy. You have never lived in the real world.'

'I may as well leave then,' I say, sulking.

'You can leave if you want. But if you do . . .'

I meet her eyes directly now, for the choices have narrowed.

'What?' I say.

'You will die.'

I am sure I will never sleep again. Stephen prescribes a bottle of Dalmane, warning that as I am extremely toxic the pills may not work. He is right. I take two and wait. Nothing. I even feel worse; I wonder if I am having a heart attack. An hour later, I take two more. Still nothing. Two more. At three a.m., I am wide awake, staring at the television set, my body throbbing and sweating and not vomiting but throwing itself up inwardly, as though my innards have been shatttered by small grenades, punctured by hawk-like shreds of bone and sinew. My hearing seems to be impaired; I can't listen to the TV though I know it is loud. By four, I have drifted into something resembling sleep.

The hue of the grey room, the stark Italian lamp, the glass brick of the table and the television are mute and inaccessible, but I know, somehow, that I am not asleep. Or not exactly. I can almost see myself as I am now, strewn across the thick white cover with my hair damp and matted, the sheets wrapped about my ankles, packets and bottles on the night table beside me; Clonidine, Tylenol, cough medicine, orange juice, *People* magazine, the empty Dalmane bottle on the floor by the bed. (When did I take the entire bottle?) There are voices inside my head; dangerous, simultaneous sounds.

... Tom Cruise was seen at L.A.'s fashionable City Café with up and coming model/actress, Australian ... party ... Have a ... posturepedic mourning ... like her nose but hated her talent ... Little Oliver Twist on his uncle's balcony, beautiful Belgravia gardens ladies and lords and merchants spinning around each other beautiful dance who will buy my sweet red roses two blooms for a penny ... O the scumbags I have to deal with ... Crilly, O Crilly, I'm leaking milk and so large, please help us, please help us, O why do they hate me? They hate me, they hate me? Geraldine, good counsellor sit with me here upon the bed, your glasses and your beautiful eyes, your face collapses into itself like a squashed spider, I scream, scream fuck, Stop! Stop! Stop! squashing, the shattering, I reach out my arms and it's shattering, shattering, and ... coyote cry shriek shriek eat the cat ... I feel the smelly soft of her rich in talcum powder, I feel the birth of her between my legs. They injected me and I had a baby. When they shot me up I thought I would die, I did die and I had the baby, the baby, yellow pig cockney O murderer man, tears a junkie's underwear and forces her to watch, O please come here and hold my wrists down, take me O take me hard and fierce, take a look at the people in *People* this week ... Maggie, I see you on the Prince of Wales Road, you're walking my way with a dealer named Sport, you are sheathed in black cloth . . . your freckles are pale and many . . . sing Billie . . . sing in my solitude you haunt me Lady Day lady day lady . . . Maggie your rag-and-bone nails . . . you are coming my way . . . a fence of barbed wire courts and crevices behind you . . . don't ring, Maggie, don't talk to my machine . . . one summer evening drunk to hell I sat there nearly lifeless . . . is Winchell home from school? I hear him, I hear him, he's crying loud obnoxious sound, the other kids don't like me, they say I'm fat and I raise my hand and the teacher doesn't call me . . . O what was that film on telly, BEAUTIFUL great big wide poppy fields, all heavenly, there was a Tory MP and his daughter was a smackthing, a Sloanie smackthing, O Tory hug your Caroline close, say I love you unconditionally, I don't care if you're a heroin addict, say . . . Goodbye to port and brandy, to vodka and the Stag, to the Smitty and the Harpic, to bottled draught and Keg! As I sat and looked at the Guinness ad, I could never figure out how your man stood up on the surfboard after fourteen pints of stout! she . . . O Crilly, O Crilly, O where the fuck are you Crilly! . . . Don't ring, Maggie, don't talk to my machine . . . Yellow pig cockney come inside of me with the windows good and steamed, hold me still I cannot move I cannot stand all this moving, fuck me. God don't let me move, sweat, piss, puke, cry, sing Goodbye to port and brandy . . . Perry's trenchcoat trailing tall . . . O lovely O lovely, they don't take te' snake out of te' bath! your face all a-crumble, O Irish mother the face of God building a co-op in te south side! O good mother look upon me, say do you believe, do you believe! That's the way we all became the Brady Bunch! Shiver shake quake quake Siobhan please forgive me, I weep beneath your cross while your boy dies in the next room, he dies now, he dies now, the room, the empty room table bed cross sing I should be so lucky lucky lucky lucky who art in heaven, hallowed by thy name . . . THE BRETS OOT NOO taking, How many buses? Flu, I've only got . . . flu . . . taking . . . Tickatickatickatickatickatickatickaticka — The Brets, the Brets, the Brets, oot noo . . . O Maggie don't ring don't talk to my machine O Perry wipe my dripping brow we will fall asleep together by the light of the paraffin heater, your hair black and dripping smack . . . *Neighbours*, everybody needs good . . . tickatickatickatickatickatickaticka . . . In Penny Lane there is a banker with a motor car, the little children laugh at him behind his back . . . the smell of sulphur in my nose, and I forgot me bloody name say the smell of pancakes and my name in batter, a Sunday smell, say never on a Sunday, a Sunday, a Sunday, then black then wood then Mommy and I rolling down that beachy green hill beyond the dunes, O the giggle of delight and laughing green hills . . . Jack, where's the fuckin' fiver you owe me? You're not me fuckin' father right! You're not me fuckin' . . . Soap star, who's a soap star . . . one summer evening . . . one summer evening drunk to hell I sat there nearly lifeless an old man on the corner sang about a thing called love . . . they drove a Mercury BMW down the Sunset Strip, Say Maggie who do you belong to, say Jezebel who do you belong to, say Bad Billy McGregor, you guys still have a potato problem up there? Get a vanload of guys take it up to Dover, hear they have pretty good seafood up there Say SiobhanSiobhanSiobhan fish and chips do you believe in Cod? THE BRETS OOT NOO Where's my tin whistle the fisherman, the fisher . . . man . . . Mommy where are you asleep Mommy where are you alive Mommy where are you are you near me are you in the house are you breathing dearly for my life are you sleeping Mommy are you sleeping Mommy won't you wake and come to me, won't you wake and tell me my name . . .

When I emerge at last from the crowded horror of my brain and being me, I am down on my knees, kneeling over the bed, my wet palms clasped together. The Dalmane bottle is empty and gaping at my feet. I have shed my nightshirt and my naked body is dripping with some sort of livid salty wet. From the mute television blares a silent MTV, a heavy metal video silently loud and thrashing, girls and guitars. The strewn debris lies in the same untidy heap, and yet I can't remember where I am. I say my name aloud to myself. Claudia. I am Claudia.

'Claudia,' I say aloud to the heavy, mouldy air, Claudia. Again. Claudia.

I don't know if we're gonna make it this time, Claudia.

On the way home from my third session with Jane, I am again silent, though the tearing in my stomach has eased. My mother stops for gas. For the first time today, I look at her. She is dressed smartly for a business lunch, her speckled hair newly cut like Louise Brooks, and she wears a white suit with red deco buttons and suede pumps of the same colour, sleek onyx earrings. I know her scent from childhood nights, my mother leaning over my bed to kiss me goodnight, the perfume lingering behind the light clink of her footsteps in the hall and the door shutting behind her, and I see her still in my tiny shut lids; Mommy in a velvet dress in the crisp Manhattan night, Mommy in a checkered taxicab, Mommy in a smoky nightclub in the West Village with her friend, watching a man with a saxophone.

'How was Jane?' she asks, as the tank is being filled.

I sit heavily in my sweat suit, thinking of a reply.

'She says I will die,' I say flatly, staring out onto Olympic Boulevard.

'She only does that to bring you down to earth. To scare you.'

'Well, she's doing a good job.'

Mama's eyes are a luminous hazel. They are shiny with tears. She reaches for me and holds me close to her. 'We're gonna make you well, baby,' she says, holding me tight, 'we're gonna make you strong.'

I let go and cry in my mother's arms.

sushi

'Your mother tells me you've been unhappy.'

In my father's presence, I eat sushi, pine for sake, cross my legs and recross them.

'Yes.' I look at my father. He is hot and stiff in a Brooks Brothers suit and tie, though it is a warm winter's day.

'She says you're seeing a therapist.'

'That's right.' What else has she told him?

'I was surprised. I thought you were fine. You look good, you've lost weight. Why are you unhappy?'

I deliberate.

'It's been a tough year.'

'Why?'

'I couldn't get out of bed.'

'Why?'

'I don't know. That's why I'm seeing a therapist. She's good. You would like her.'

'Was it England?'

'England . . . No. I love England.'

'Will you go back?'

'Eventually.'

Behind the counter the chef carves slices of baked anago eel, heaped on rectangles of rice with great precision. I am impressed, even hungry.

'When you do go back?' my father says, 'maybe I'll buy you a new car.'

'That would be lovely.'

'We can go to the races on Wednesday if you like.'

'I'd enjoy that.'

We eat. I take a sip of diet Coke with ice and lemon. I gulp it down as though it were whiskey. When I look up at my father's face, he is old and puzzled and sad.

rafi

I attend NA meetings. Randomly. I explore the obscure corners of the city rather than remaining local. They tell me that sober living is more surreal than anything, that being awake is the only true psychedelia. I search out the weirdness of my native town through the weirdness of its meetings. The greater the distance, the greater the difference. I am desperate to make a *difference*. When I am less dizzy, when my skin has toughened, I brave Hollywood meetings, allowing myself to be seen and recognised, even to be addressed by name. The brazen warmth of new Americans bewilders me; the use of so many superlatives such as GREAT and REVOLTING, the shameless cheek of rising tones, an exuberance that is vivid like new pennies. CLAUDIA I'M DELIGHTED TO SEE YOU, an NA local dares to say, a man whom I've met once. And they tell me how well I'm doing. And they shove matchbooks with telephone numbers scrawled in them into my palm, saying, phone anytime, phone anytime. I'm not sure what to make of it. Their acceptance daunts me. I blush at their embraces and shy from the meetings in which there seems a danger of being liked, as though to ward off the inevitable, the disillusionment which follows intimacy. I do not trust the 'love in these rooms', the paper plates heaped with cookies and fat-free pineapple cake, the blinding cigarette smoke, the recognition of me and the astounding memory of my own words mirrored by crowds. Yet I eat the cake, I smoke like a chimney, I attend meetings. Every day, everywhere.

I find solace at the Chemical Dependence Center in West Hollywood. I like the cosy disfunction of this room; the twitchy floorboards, the soda machine that never works, the pimply, volatile man at the desk. And the permanant schedule of AA and NA meetings chalked upon a blackboard in powder blue. And the grey rug dotted with cigarette burns and auditorium chairs strewn by the door, before the big dirty windows, beside the bathroom and the podium. I like the midnight meetings; boisterous, candlelit, absurd. The witching hour frees me, always. It unleashes my voice, it soothes my bed-chafed skin with its honeyed light. Stuffed between two brash neon bars in the dead centre of Boystown, it is invaded by noise from the street; a throb of disco from Rage, metal music from cars, the cries of loud camp men, the motorcycles, the sirens and circular shadows from police cars. Staring from behind the murky double window, I see it all: the pink and yellow of cursive neon signs, Rage, Key Largo, L.A. Gear, muscles fastened with shiny black leather, fluorescent jumpsuits, tank tops baring shoulders, men of all sizes, all ages.

Tonight I climb the stairs with a sense of dread. I feel stupid and small and squeaky. Perhaps I have overstayed my welcome here; I may suddenly be unliked, unrecognised, ignored. The novelty of me will wear off, as novelty does.

The place is packed with regulars; the wiry ones, the withered ones, the cosy, craggy regulars reminding me of old soil or worn camping knives. I suddenly feel I have too many voices, too many homes, too many thoughts and no bravado. I crawl into the candlelit and smoke-stained room, a den of ex-vice, an accidental living-room. I take my seat in the middle. This feels adventurous; usually I am off to the side.

And O it is crowded like Friday night, though the addicts are less rambunctious than they usually are at midnight meetings;

more intent, attuned. They watch the speaker with interest. And I am late.

I am greeted by two straight and older balding moustached men. One says, you're looking better, Claudia. Real good. I try to remember his name.

I relax. The speaker is a pock-marked, slick-haired Chicano with a fine chunk of sobriety behind him. His voice is deep and strong. He speaks with the glee of a man who knows the audience are his.

'. . . You know like when you're loaded, you wanna try it on everyone? If the fucking cat walks by, you'll blow that shit in the cat's face. Well my uncle got me stoned when I was eight years old. I couldn't smoke on a joint without choking, so my uncle and all his friends just blew smoke in a bag and laid it on me. I wondered . . . you see, I lived with my grandparents and my uncle. My grandfather was the meanest son of a bitch in town, and when he used to yell at me I'd be so freaked out I couldn't speak. But I started noticing that when he yelled at my uncle, my uncle was real cool . . .' (Rafi shuts his eyes and nods his head to demonstrate.) 'He just fucking stood there with his great old mean eyes shut, cool as ice. I envied him something rotten. I wanted to be just like him. I noticed that he kept going to the bathroom. One day I followed him and pushed the door open. What I saw was works and blood. I said, let me try it Frank. Let me. So he said (imitating cool nodding head) You . . . want to junior? And he got it together to stick that fucker in my arm. I won't ever forget that first time. We sat on the front lawn with spare tyres all over the fucking dead grass and the dogs, all mutt and ugly, wandering around us. We didn't give a shit. We was fucking beautiful. My uncle says to me, you want . . . some ice-cream . . . Rafi? And my mouth explodes like. I heard the ding-a-ling of the ice-cream truck. I wanted that ice-cream bad.

Somehows I end up in the street and I thought I would take it on myself to yell for that truck to stop. I stood there like this — imitating himself nodding, smacked up — and I said "Wait" real fucking quiet. I thought I was yelling. The truck had to stop 'cause I was right in front of the fucker. I bought myself one of them push-up things and I settled down on that dead grass. Of course what ended up happening, I would sit with my head all nodded out over my knees and the ice-cream pushed out over the lid, and those skinny scoundrel dogs come and lick the stuff till it was gone.'

The others are laughing, and I laugh, but the image haunts me and makes me sad. A young hippie with lanky hair glances at me every time something funny is said. There is much smiling between us; we 'shine' in affinity, though fuck knows why. I feel hot from the pit of my chest to my feet, and I take off my sweater leaving my shoulders bare.

Rafi is quick and fire-eyed now, gesticulating in the air, frantic.

'If you guys think well, "I haven't reached my bottom yet" you know you're fooling yourselves because this *is* the bottom, just being in NA. We're as low as we can get and we're fucking grateful to be that way. We have everything we need at the bottom, with the other doper drunken bottomers. What I want to tell you is, there ain't nothing wrong with doing drugs. Not a goddarned thing in the world. There ain't nothing wrong with doing drugs, as long as you don't know about Narcotics Anonymous. The way you fucked up is, you let yourself find out! You fuckheads! Now you ain't never gonna be free!'

We roar, all of us roar, with laughter.

·

'And you're so stupid, you couldn't even think of your own logo!' He points to the NA logo, which is similar to the AA logo. 'You had to steal it from the winos! And "Sniff" Anonymous, they're really stupid, just think what a dickhead you have to be to do that shit in the first place? Like when it's heroin and you're getting busted by the police, you don't think nothing, just "I wish these guys would keep their voices down". But on that Peruvian shit, you're sitting there all night just waiting for those fuckers to arrive!' More laughter.

'The first time I hear about AA, I'm doin' time at San Quentin, and an announcement gets made over the speaker: AA meeting in game room. I says to my buddy, "What the fuck is American Airlines doing at San Quentin?" So he explains what AA is, and I say, "I'm not having none of that shit. I'm one of the meanest mothers in prison; I have all the dope, booze, frills I need." My friend tries to tempt me, saying "They'll be cake there." "Fuck you," I says back to him. "I have the whole stash of cake and cookies."

'So he says, "They'll be girls there," and I says "Where do I sign?" I go that meeting and two beautiful chicks are sitting right there on the panel. I don't hear a damn thing anyone says. I crouch in my seat so I could get a good look, up their skirts, you know, and later I tell my friend "They were blue an' I'm happy." The stupid thing is, now there is a permanant AA mark by my name. This asshole prison guard comes up the next week and opens the gate, saying "It's time for your AA meeting." "Fuck you," I says, and shut the gate, but it slides open on me. "I have you marked for the meetings," says the guard, and I say "fuck you" and shut that fucker again, but it slides open a second time, and then a third. So I go to that meeting and there isn't one girl there, not one fucking girl. So I'm released in a couple of weeks and I start drinking and slamming dope like I never have before. But now, whenever I do it, these stupid little phrases sneak into my brain, no matter how fucked up I am, like "easy does it" or "let go and let God". Fuck! I was blown, destroyed!'

I am smoking furiously. The pleasant-faced hippie (forgot all about him) asks me for a light.

'Two years later,' continues Rafi, 'I'm going to these meetings twice a day and I come back for my uncle. I find him one day, trespassing on a neighbour's back lawn, lying butt naked with a girl I ain't never met before. The two of them are nodding and itching like crazy. They're all pinned to death with filthy hair. I says to my uncle, "Come on man, there's an NA meeting on the next street over, come with me." Now at this time in my life there was one thing I couldn't stand and that was a bitch fucked up on smack. My uncle don't say nothing but the bitch says, "What . . . is NA?" I tell her, "Shut up bitch!" and turn back to my uncle, saying "Hey man you've got to come, you just have to show up, I'll take you." But my uncle don't say nothing; just sits doubled over with his hair in his face. But the bitch says, "What . . . time . . . does it start?" So I push her and I yell, "Shut up bitch!" and I says again to my uncle, "I'll drive you there and drive you back. You don't have to be clean to go." My uncle starts to open his eyes but ends up nodding again with his lids down to his ankles. And he's itching, slowly, like wherever he scratches ain't the place he itches. Finally he says, "No . . . No thanks, man." But the bitch, that naked bitch, leans in close to me and says, "I'll go". Two months later my uncle ODs and dies. But that girl has been sober from that day onwards. I meant to twelve-step my uncle and instead God puts the bitch in my path. Today she is my wife.'

Rafi motions to a skinny, painted woman in heavy eye make-up and a purple halter top. She smiles and raises her hand in a lazy half-wave.

I am tired at halftime, I need to leave. Randy is there in a plaid jacket and new bleached haircut, running about, hugging and talking to people. He has four weeks of clean time, as I have. But he has made more friends. He is less shy. It makes me feel inadequate. He hugs me. I see Jean, lean and pretty under a sheet of straight hair and a pink camisole. More hugging. On my way out, the hippie of the continual smile approaches me and introduces himself, asking how much time do I have, where am I from, what is my drug of choice? There is talk of coffee at Canter's. But my flesh trembles with the after-sting of caffeine, and Rafi's pitch twists in my belly like a rusty stick shift when it is jerked forward against its will. I hold my car keys in the air; I'll just go home.

But my name is called, and the caller calls from somewhere else. I turn but I don't see him. I turn the other way and Bob is there, my old school friend, grinning into the boyish, freckled flatness of his face. I embrace him, without thinking, holding him close. I laugh. He laughs.

'Why aren't you in San Francisco?' I cry.

'Nobody knows I'm down here,' he explains. 'Don't tell my mom.'

'Where have you come from now?'

Bob motions vaguely to one of the clubs.

Bob and I have always shared a love for stupid, hysterical things: fluorescent supermarkets at four in the morning, monster-sized boxes of laundry detergent, a psychedelic montage from a film about cells shown in chemistry, the lined and earnest face of a math teacher, the shrillness of a classmate's voice after coughing.

We eat Chinese chicken salad at a shiny bistro in the valley. We sit among white-shirted, mini-skirted, and tidy-haired patrons. We watch the other diners and we are silent, misplaced.

When Bob is nervous, he holds his head stiffly as though

aiming to make it parallel with his neck. He speaks in a monotone.

'I'm having some doubts about my sexuality.' He breaks the silence. We look at another. 'I think I might be gay.'

'Really? Have you slept with a man?'

'Kind of. I've . . . been doing it for years, actually. Remember when I visited you in England? Remember Todd? He was my . . . lover. Remember Don? And I'm sort of seeing someone right now. His name is Louis.'

I begin to laugh. Presently, Bob laughs. We laugh together for a good long time.

'It makes perfect sense,' I say at last.

'Why?'

'I don't know. Because it does. Hey Bob, listen. Listen to me. You are gay and I'm a junkie.'

'You are?'

'Uh huh.'

'You never told me.'

'I dropped clues.'

'Cocaine?'

'Heroin.'

We laugh some more. It is really terribly, terribly funny. I watch his laughing baby eyes; they glaze and narrow gleefully.

'Who would have thought it?' he says.

We pay our bill and drive through Laurel Canyon to the tip of Grandview Drive, a path on the edge of a cliff. When I first moved to L.A. almost fifteen years ago, we lived here, in a rare old cabin of a house built solely of oak. It had an old fireplace and a master window perched steeply above the dive of the mountain. Beneath it were large cactuses and further down, the city sprawled like an airport runway before bursting into neon strips of road, high and low buildings, wide rectangular suburbs, and eventually a luminous flirting strip of sea. The house has since burnt to the ground in a brush fire, but the view is the same, especially on this night, this fine and crisp and clear night. Bob and I sit in Bob's old car, gazing at L.A. as we would from a high tower or helicopter. Bob has made a compilation cassette; a collection of television soundtracks — *Jeopardy*, *Bewitched*, *Love American Style*. Herb Alpert plays now; 'Tijuana Brass'. All at once stark and surreal, giddy and silent, solitary and together, we sit like twin towers painted pink and silly, together, while the city twinkles in the sameness of night, beyond that empty lot of embers.

I have a pap smear on Wednesday. My first in years. The gynaecologist is a smooth young woman from Calcutta, though she speaks with a Californian accent. I am wary. She knows it. My body is stiff and inhospitable. Without Crilly or heroin, the spreading of my legs feels pointless. I apologise in advance for the tensing of my hips and pelvis, ensuring that it will be so. The tongs are like an army, an iron storm of soldiers, scissors. The ceiling is clean and plain, white as a place without life. 'Relax', says the gentle doctor, who is my own age or younger. 'Relax'.

The office is on the sixteenth floor. The view is one spectacular sprawl of road and little boxes, though the day is not clear. I lie with my legs up over L.A. I do not relax.

She tests me for a host of venereal diseases. She examines me for ovarian cancer. The smear is not my main reason for being there. She understands. I am two months off the smack, one month and a half off methadone, twenty-one days off everything else, the frills. It's a good time to know whether I'll die or not.

'All I've done is retch,' I said to my friend Bob. 'Now I want to revel.'

'In what?' he asked.

What indeed. Life probably, I think.

After the smear, a receptionist takes two hundred dollars from me and sends me to a lower floor. I ride the elevator down with an odd stranger, a twisted and mutated kind of man. Incorrect buttons are pushed. We stop at one or two floors that have nothing to do with either of us. No one gets in.

The basement is notably less expensive than the sixteenth floor, laid with linoleum instead of carpet, and mean steel numbers on corridor doors. I pray while meandering, zigzagging as I go, on that clinky floor of grey and white. I find the lab and turn its knob.

A girl sits at a desk. She wears a T-shirt saying 'LA Specs' in primary colours. She is thin with long hair and a narrow, jutting jaw. Her skin is not dark but bronzed and shiny. She looks up.

'You're too young to be here,' she says. I am not flattered.

'I'm not,' I retort.

'Yes you are. You're under sixteen or eighteen.'

'There's no minimum age to be tested for AIDS. Besides, I'm twenty-five.'

'Oh. That's amazing. The movies could use a face like yours.'

'I think they have more faces than they could spit on.' I don't feel comfortable with this analogy, but I don't bother to retract it. What does she mean, 'the movies could use a face like yours?' Just because I look young? Is this good? Or does she think I am some sort of facial dwarf?

The technician rises from her desk and stretches. A *People* magazine falls to the floor. It is an exclusive. Its cover reads in gold script: Predictions for the Ten Hottest People of 1990. She takes me into the next room.

'You're really brave to do this,' she tells me. 'I could never do it.'

'Thank you.'

She sits down and pushes up my sleeve. The room is large, with one window. There is no view but the sky is white as stucco and blinding besides. Test-tubes are everywhere. It's a real lab. Authentic. The girl natters.

'Are you English?' she asks.

'No. I live there.'

'My boyfriend is English. He comes from Hull.' She prepares the syringe.

'I knew a man from Hull. He was a train-spotter,' I say.

But the girl is busy with needles and things.

'Does your boyfriend have a northern accent?' I ask.

'You mean like Oregon or something?'

'No. I mean the north of England.'

'I don't think so. He doesn't sound like the Beatles. He doesn't sound like he's from Liverpool.'

'Well, he wouldn't, coming from Hull.'

'He mumbles a lot, though.'

'They all do,' I say, meaninglessly.

I cannot keep my eyes off the needle. It is fierce. She notices my discomfort. 'It's a good thing you don't like these things,' she says. 'That means you won't do drugs.'

'I've done them anyway.'

'Yeah, Most English people do —'

'I'm not English.'

'But you sound it. My boyfriend does a lot of drugs. Do you ever go the Power Station?'

'No. What's that?' In it goes, the bloodsucker. I cringe. She wriggles it around.

'It's a club where all the English guys hang out. That's where I met my boyfriend. Only you might not get in 'cause you look so young.'

'What kind of drugs does your boyfriend do?'

'You know, the norm, coke and speed and stuff.'

I am disappointed. I watch the clear coil. 'Got it,' says the girl. The blood is wagon red and it speeds like a demon back to the test-tube. 'I was surprised,' she continues, 'at how decadent he is. Like I would have left him a long time ago, but he loves to fuck. I mean he really loves to.'

'That's good,' I say. She withdraws the needle and packs the tube in a case marked with my pseudonym. I have chosen the name 'Pamela Watkins', because I miss Pamela. The lab assistant seems to have finished talking. 'Goodbye,' I say. 'It was nice to meet you.'

'Goodbye,' she says absently, fiddling with something small inside her hand.

I'm so hot on my way home and full of a frenzy which keeps my shirt creased in the elbows and beneath my damp breasts, while stockings rub and chafe with a grasshopper sound against my thighs. Sunset Strip is swarming with tripods and television crew men. I pass a dozen billboards of big Hollywood faces, guns and wetsuits. I cannot bear the traffic; a brazen team of Mercedes gleaming in the premature winter sun. There is no breeze.

As I reach Laurel, the air cools with the leafy overspill from Laurel Canyon, all green, and I think about acoustic guitars and tapestries strewn luxuriantly in trees or in shady oak houses, a mile or so into the canyon, ten or twenty years behind. The road is clear. I pass Ryan Buck's house where the ugly old Caddy sits shrill and alight. Ryan Buck was my first ever boyfriend. I have seen him at meetings. He has ten years of sobriety now. He is always proselytising, preaching to me about the twelve steps. He reminds me that he was the first man I ever did drugs with. I tell him that that was only cocaine and I hated it. Crilly was really the first. What's more, Crilly is twice the man stoned that he is sober. He says I am in denial.

Atop of the stucco steps, beneath a Spanish awning, Ryan sprawls in his chair, shirtless and sun-loving. The look of his chest and the bandana about his head jolts me into an agitated *déjà vu*; this is Ryan as he was a decade before, as he was when I met him on a pleasant and splintery stage beneath those careless repertory beams.

He gazes vaguely now in the direction of the sun. I know he is poorly from a motor bike collision. One of many, the stupid fuck. Before the light turns green, I engage in a fantasy of violence, wherein I might hurl his battered body to the bottom of the stairs and watch him gape on the hard, stained ground, cut and bleeding as he would be.

I press the gas with the intent to speed, but the light is still a bastard red. I screech to my right and onto Fairfax and an older stretch of Sunset where boys in short shorts sell their bodies on street corners. Their silhouettes shiver at night in front of the International House of Pancakes. They're gone now. And traffic has lightened.

To my relief, nobody is home. I throw my things upon the floor. I leap to the cabinet and eat most of my brother's chocolate chip cookies. To compensate, I prepare myself a bowl of tuna fish mixed with Weight Watchers mayonnaise, enjoying the tigerish sister cats as they rub against my legs. I soon reel from the after-taste of low-cal mayo, and I give the rest to the cats. I finish my brother's cookies.

'Are there any newcomers?' asks the leader of Elana's Al-anon meeting. I speak my name, cutting myself short before saying 'And I'm an addict'.

'Hello, Claudia,' they say, in unison, 'welcome.'

I giggle. This is a prosperous meeting; full of suede and festive pumps. We're in Westwood. People laugh at things I don't think are funny. One man says, 'I know there's a recession on, but not in my reality.' For the first time in weeks, I wish I was stoned. Someone's brought a puppy. It tumbles about on the rug chewing people's shoes and styrofoam cups. He has my undivided attention.

Each person's pitch is timed with a cooking timer, three minutes. I want to interrupt, to yell about different varieties of hash: Moroccan, black, Lebanese. I am uncomfortable in the oversoft settee; I sink into its fold. When nearly everyone has shared and there is time left to spare, I talk about Crilly, mentioning that I am an addict as well. (I'm no victim, dickheads, I'm a parasite, the sort you hate and adore, the reason you're here in the first place.) At the end of the meeting, I am not approached with votes of faith and embraces. I am only given one phone number, from the girl who owns the puppy.

Elana and I have coffee at Canter's. Elana asks how I liked the meeting. Elana is an old friend; I've known her since I was twelve. We've shared drama classes, dance classes, diets.

'It was nice,' I say. 'You must remember, I'm spoiled. I'm used to people coming up to me afterwards and welcoming me. As a newcomer, I mean. And it was a bit homogenous.'

'What does that mean?'

'Everyone looked the same.'

'Oh. Well, I guess that's because it's Westwood.'

'And also, I got the feeling that people were looking down on me. Because I'm an addict and not just a victim.'

'But we have a lot of double-winners at Al-anon.'

'Yes, but they're probably valium addicts or something.' I return to my earlier objection. 'At your typical AA or NA meeting,' I say, 'we get a variety of faces. Poor and rich, black and white and Mexican, yuppies, street people and pop stars, handicapped people and actors, vagrants and agents, lawyers and waiters.'

'Oh,' says Elana.

'You name it,' I say. 'I don't like feeling like I'm in a room full of only professionals. I wouldn't mind some professionals. But I was getting claustrophobic.'

'Oh. Well, sorry.'

'It isn't your fault,' I say. 'Anyway, I shouldn't criticise your home meeting. There were some good things. I enjoyed what

that one guy said, with the long hair; it was all just a bit
. . . homogenous.'

'I keep thinking of milk when you say "homogenous". Like
"homogenised".'

I ignore this. I am too swelled up inside my own arrogance, a
kind of strangled lie, but I can't see to temper it.

I go on, 'Perhaps you should branch out a bit. Perhaps you
should go to other Al-anon meetings, just to see what they're
like.'

'I've been meaning to,' says Elana. 'But as you know, I hardly
have any time. I work all day, I have choir on Monday, my
Debtors Anonymous on Tuesday, Thursday is the only time I
can get to the gym . . .'

'Oh, Elana, you could do it if you really wanted to. You would
make the time. For instance, you told me last week you weren't
going to see Burt and you've seen him twice since then. You
could tell Burt to fuck off and fit in more meetings if you really
wanted to.'

Elana looks defeated. 'I know,' she says. 'I'm a creature of
habit. It's hard for me to break routine. And though I'm still
confused in my feelings for Burt, I miss the attention when I
don't have it.'

'You shouldn't fuse your whole identity into any old asshole
who looks at you sideways. You deserve better.'

'I know,' she says. She is ashen. And I am being a bit of a prick.

I eat half of Elana's French fries. Our waitress, unlike the
ludicrously endowed, bleached and volatile veterans, is new to
the scene. She is a pretty rotund thing with great green eyes and
a rosebud mouth. She clearly hails from somewhere vast and
innocent; Idaho or somewhere. Titillated by my friend's fries, I
order another plate. My tights are bothering me. I take them off,
along with my shoes. My legs, now bare beneath the table, put

me in a better humour. Inspired, Elana removes her stilettos and places them beside her. The manager approaches and requests that she put them back on. My own bare feet and legs are concealed in the generous gauze of my skirt. I take pleasure in getting away with something. I sit cross-legged with my flesh pressed against the red booth vinyl. Red vinyl always reminds me of childhood; the Gold Rail Brasserie where my father flirted with the waitress, where I ate hamburgers, French fries, Coke. Above the formica, I maintain the poise of a woman who has her shoes on.

My fries are late. Canter's is absurdly bright like the inside of a refrigerator. The ceiling glares in backlit madness, hosting swirly screaming reds, oranges and yellows: Colours to be wired by while drinking instant coffee in the wee hours. Colours to be hungry by. Orange is the colour of concession stands in suburban cinemas, alive with the smell and cackle of buttered popcorn. Yellow is Sunday brunch, a happy colour, or the frost of a toddler's icing on a bloated yellow birthday cake. Red is . . .

Our yellow-haired waitress comes upon us with a plate of fries. She says that due to the delay, the fries are on the house. I wonder whether she is paying for them out of her own pocket. I feel a flush of tenderness for her and devour them, to please her.

Elana and I discuss the fellowship, mothers and waitresses. She's a good friend to me. She's the kind of friend who sends cards when I've got the flu. (Not even my mother does this.) If she were English she would have one of those London secretary voices. She would wear pastel minis and button down jumpers. She would ride the top half of buses and talk to her mates about *Home and Away*, and her boyfriend Brad who works down the estate agents.

More probably she would be nothing like this.

The old-time waitresses mill about behind counters and between booths. They share varicose veins and their hair is teased high and tired. They have martyred, misshapen bodies and they wear uniforms the colour of margarine.

It is not yet midnight. Elana's tired. I'm not. I'll catch a candlelight meeting.

And crowded it is, for a Wednesday. The upstairs annex is textured with smoke. The late night smokers assemble themselves in the west side of the room. I sit with them, for I am now a smoker. I love to smoke. I'm almost proud of it. We use rusty coffee cans for ashtrays. The room, lit solely by an overhanging bulb, smells faintly of humidity; the last stale trace of an earlier rain.

The speaker is English. He's called Jamie Todd and he's from Bournemouth. I have seen his pitch before. He drops names of rock and roll stars whenever he can.

'I never understood the expression "drug of choice",' he tells us. 'Like I never went to my dealer and went, "Oy mate have you got my drug of choice?" My drug of choice was more. My drug of choice was yours!'

An addict claps his hands. 'Oh, don't clap on your own,' chortles Jamie. 'Someone'll throw you a fish!'

A latecomer cackles loudly.

'Also,' he continues, 'I never knew what the fuck a blackout was. Like, I never knew that I had had blackouts about, say, two hundred times. What's more, I never knew that you actually did stuff during a blackout, such as travel. One evening I'd be drinking pints in Barking, next thing I knew I would wake up in Spain. I can't remember one fucking thing I ever did during a blackout. But I do know that I never did anything nice, like give a child a toy.'

When the meeting adjourns, I drink herb tea at the Greenery with my new friend Randy. We sit outside beneath a flapping canopy in the middle of Boystown. Regulars emerge late from the centre, meeting our eyes as they stroll by. 'Hey!' yells Jimmy K., who is dark and wiry with under-eye shadows and a long pony tail, 'Read my shirt!' The shirt reads 'Shut Up Bitch'. I try to figure it out. Is he telling me to shut up, though I have not spoken once during the entire meeting? Randy is equally perplexed. He did share at the meeting; perhaps the shirt is meant for him. I breathe a sigh of relief and order doughnuts for the both of us. Across from us, two boys in matching polo shirts meet us with a shrug. 'What was *that*?' they exclaim in incredulous sympathy.

Randy is a quick confider. He tells me that he is HIV positive, and he does not believe that he will die. He doesn't dwell on it. He confesses that he is also an obsessive-compulsive. I ask him what he means.

'I'm constantly worried that someone I know or care about will die,' he explains. 'And I am always counting to myself. It's like a superstitious thing. Like if I don't get to ten by the time the truck passes someone nice will die. Or if I don't get to eight before the second time the telephone rings, my boyfriend will be unfaithful.'

'I do things like that,' I say. 'I always need to touch things, objects.' I touch the salt shaker and the cap, which are made of different substances. I touch the pitcher of hot water, the napkin, and the saucer.

'I'm afraid that if I don't touch these things,' I say, 'that I will never find success in my life. There is a tree growing by the steps to my house. I always have to touch it on the way in. And I always have to touch the leaves.'

We discuss Freud's *The Rat Man*. Randy and I agree that we do these things to fend off death. 'Claudia,' he says, leaning into my face, 'you are probably an obsessive-compulsive as well.'

I take a sip of my cranberry-apple tea.

'I knew it,' I say.

Upon leaving Randy and the Greenery in Boystown, I realise that I have lost my ring. I was fiddling with it at Canter's, along with my tights and shoes. It is late; around four. I park my car in the lot and clink my heels in a pacy way, glancing at Mortimer's Flea Market and the Kosher butcher's shop, boarded up as though they have never seen the light of day. Outside Mortimer's, a dusty, dreadlocked black man plays a Burt Bacharach medley on a xylophone-type thing. He wears a suit so starched and ancient that it will not move with the contours of his body.

The young waitress is still on her shift. When I tell her I have lost my ring, she tears into the cracks of the booth looking for it. She checks under the table and beneath the seats. I try to tell her that it doesn't matter, but she won't listen. She finds nothing. She turns to face me, her eyes enormous with empathy. 'Could you have left it in your car?' she asks.

'I don't think so.'

'Have you checked your bag thoroughly?' Her accent is almost southern by now.

'Yes.'

'That's terrible,' she says. I am certain that she will cry. 'Was it a gift?'

'No,' I lie, 'I bought it at a garage sale in Glendale. It's not sentimental or anything. It's nothing really. It's just a ring. Please don't worry.' I feel the need to reassure her. I touch her shoulder. 'Really,' I say, feeling strange and powerless.

On Thursday morning, I phone for my results. They are not ready. I attend a yoga class. I aspire to serenity through a series of contortions, but my head is fraught with static. 'If thoughts of the outside world come into your head,' advises the teacher, 'just pluck them as you would a weed from a garden. If you hear noises from outside, just think of them as the mantra of the universe and then forget them.'

I think about this, but end up considering the weeds themselves and then gardening and eventually a gardening show I have seen called *Tell It Green* on British morning television, and then poppies, blue and bulbous, before they are ripe. I try breathing deeply and listening to the deep, even heaving of those around me, those who are stretching and serene. I attempt a back-lift with my legs bent against the wall. A strain of rap music tears through the window, from a stationary car. I gyrate lightly.

> I got a rhyme
> that I think you need to know
> about a funky little bitch
> with tits as white as snow
> Got a girlfriend name of Kim
> A boyfriend name of Chuck
> With the girl she loves to rim
> and the boy she loves to fuck
> I says girl you need a man
> who won't take none of that dyke shit
> so get your white ass over here
> and upon my face you'll sit
> She says Nigger I don't care
> if you got a cucumber or a clit
> the way I see it, Kim's left thumb
> is bigger than your dick . . .

At least they flow, those words, they flow. I'm grateful for a rhythm. I try to muffle the rap in my head, but the groove persists even after the tune has ended. I wonder what the car looks like. I think of a Buick with low suspension. The sun sheds a smoggy blob of light into the room. The breathing is still and heavy around me.

If I have AIDS, I think, as the class draws to a close in a chant of breathy oms, if I have it, I will never have to do this again.

I spot a fellow recovering addict across the room. I have seen her at a women's NA meeting. In the dressing-room, we say hello to one another. I notice that she is wearing the same spotted dress she wore at the women's meeting.

I buy a diet Coke in a liquor store on the other side of Larchmont. I rush past jugs of wine and liquor. If I have AIDS, I think, I may start drinking, really drinking, so that I can be like one of those crazy lushes I'm always hearing about, barhopping, blackouting, committing severe criminal acts in the tiniest hours of the night and forgetting all about it by the sooty light of dawn. And then I think, I never really did drink, why do I have to give up everything, as if the desire to drink is dormant within me somewhere, just because I'm a junkie without her junk? How can they be sure I'm so desperate to fill the gap? To hell with them! If I have AIDS I will prove the pricks right and crumble down beneath the low shade of a bar-room stool. I will write Hemingway-esque novels about drinking and bullfights and learn to sing songs about lowdown boozers and lamp-posts, like Tom Waits. I pay for my diet Coke, resisting a fudge sample on the counter. Life is riddled with temptation. I might never live to see the half of it. I am a pussyfoot junkie. I never did fuck-all. I still cringe at the sight of a needle. I have never tried 'Dylodded', sold myself or robbed a drugstore. I did nothing but lie among mildewy sheets with the blinds drawn, waiting and watching Australian soap operas the whole day long . . .

I wonder if this is my life flashing before me — the frank, abbreviated version. The street is wide and very light. I spot the NA girl in her spotted dress, emerging from the Yoga Centre across the street. I worry. What if she has seen me coming out of the liquor store and assumed I've purchased booze? I take my diet Coke from its paper bag, making sure to crackle it as I do, as though she could hear it. I rumple the bag and throw it towards a waste bin. I miss. I hold the Coke at chest's length as I walk. My efforts are pointless, as the spotted woman clearly does not see me.

I phone the doctor. 'We do not have your results yet,' says the receptionist, exasperated. I apologise and say I will phone later.

In the afternoon, I attend an AA crosstalk meeting in a park recreation centre. I have never been to crosstalk before, though I know they are of a more conversational format, less formal than most AA meetings. I am fascinated. I almost forget about the chilling threat of my own blood.

'I have relapsed,' divulges a sunken man with a tired moustache. 'I had a drink. Six years of sobriety . . . gone.'

The pale man weeps, stooped like a turtle into the table. A burly friend sits beside him, patting his shoulder.

'Why did you relapse?' challenges a man from across the room. The asker is a brisk man in a blue suit, with a bundled sleeping baby in his arms. He looks like a game show host, apart from the sleeping baby.

'I don't know,' replies the weeping drinker. Nobody speaks. The room, beige with metal auditorium chairs, is silent but for the squeaks and sobs of the relapser.

'What you should perhaps look at,' says an Englishman in a white shirt, 'is that a slip begins way before the drink. What has been happening in your life?'

'Well,' ponders the drinker. 'Nothing really . . . work, well, no worse than usual. I broke up with my girlfriend, but I don't really like her anyway . . . or maybe I do and I'm just in denial . . . fuck, I don't know . . .'

'Have you been speaking with your sponsor?' asks the game show host.

'No. But I don't really like him anyway. Or I can't figure out if I don't like him or if he doesn't like me. Fuck, I don't know. I just saw the bar, and I thought, gee . . . one won't really . . . shit, I smelled it like, and I knew there was no turning back!'

'You know,' begins a large black man in a slow and tender alto, 'you must not judge yourself too harshly. In a way, it's good that this has happened —'

'What the hell —' begins game show host.

'It's good that this has happened. It forces us all, each and every one of us, you included and especially, to realise that we are never free of the disease —'

'What the hell is that?' The game show host is irate. 'That's what meetings are for! You don't need to go out on the programme to realise that you're an alcoholic.'

The black man is unruffled. He continues. ''Cause the disease never leaves us and we must always remember who we are, even if it means going out sometimes, because none of us here is perfect, we are only human, we are God's children and we share a fatal disease, we are here to —'

'Look,' cuts in the game show host, 'if you're diligent about prayer and meditation, and you read —'

'Listen,' says the black man loudly, 'I'm sick to death of you cutting in on me, always interrupting, why don't you just shut up!'

'I *wasn't* interrupting, I was just saying —'

'You *were* interrupting, Milton, I hate to be the one to say it.'

'That's right, Milton,' agrees the wispy woman, 'you always interrupt.'

Milton sulks.

'We share an affinity,' continues the black man. 'And that is what brings us together.'

Looking around, I notice that I am only one of two women. In AA meetings, there seem to be more men than women. I consider going to AA more than NA. Surely, they won't mind if I come to AA? Drugs and alcohol are more or less the same, anyway. I don't really like all the NA meetings; too many tattoos and leather jackets, it feels like something I've been through already. Through the windows, men play tennis on the west side of the park, basketball on the east side. Vagrants wander by; a brown-clad woman weighed down by stacks of newspaper, an old man pushing a shopping cart full of fast food wrappers and broken shoes. Across the table from me sits Fred, an ancient and hollow-eyed man so ravaged that he can barely stand, though he does so often, shuffling across the room to help himself to paper plates of vanilla wafers from the kitchen counter.

Encouraged by the previous speaker, Fred speaks now.

'Yeah,' he says, in a slurred and toothless way, 'we'll always accept you. We love you. I slip. I've slipped many times. I'll probably slip again, 'cause I'm an alcoholic. That's jus' who I am. I am your brother. You know when you slip that you can tell anyone in this whole room. You can call me or anyone. Just like if I slip, I know I can call someone . . .'

'Don't call me,' says Milton.

'Perhaps you ought to pay more attention to the sponsor issue,' advises the Englishman, gently.

But the drinker, whose name is Mike, is silent and ashen.

'Fuck, Mike,' shouts a fattish man from the right-hand corner of the room, 'let's get real here. This isn't some half-assed feeble predicament. Look at yourself. Have you really been working your programme?'

'I think so,' whispers Mike.

'What?'

'I think . . . that I have been.'

'Have you been reading or re-reading the big book of Alcoholics Anonymous?'

'Yes.'

'What page are you on?'

I can take it no longer. 'For fuck's sake,' I yell, louder than I'd intended, 'don't berate him. He's not here to be abused by the likes of you. Do you always make a note of what page you are on every time you read the big book?'

'As a matter of fact, I do,' says the fat man, smugly. 'And I always make a note to read page 449, especially if I think I'm gonna go out.'

'We're not berating him,' pipes up the man's wife, who strongly resembles him, 'we're just trying to get real, here.'

I haven't noticed her before. So there are three women here. I am the youngest. Quite a few of the men are giving me the eye, I notice. I forget about Mike's relapse for a while. I catch my reflection in a teaspoon, but I can make out nothing but skin and an eye stretched in the pewter of the utensil. I touch my face. I have good skin, I think. I have always had good skin. And I have never used needles. Very few women are infected, even now. I am probably not infected. I gaze at the Englishman. He is much older, attractive. He sounds like he could be from Essex or somewhere.

Mike's relapse takes up most of the meeting. In the last few minutes, Milton shares.

'I don't know how to say this,' he begins, his head still still and stoic but his eyes, glassy. 'My sister has AIDS.'

Several sighs of sympathy emanate from the room, but no one comments. The secretary, who wears glasses and a green sweater, interjects. 'I'm afraid that's all the time we have. Please grab someone after the meeting if you haven't gotten what you need.'

Milton hangs his head and attends to his baby, who is beginning to stir. I feel cheated for him. Couldn't we stay for ten more minutes, to discuss the sister with AIDS? It all seems disproportionate.

Some of us stay to help with chairs and tables. The Essex man and I are among the stayers. He asks where I am from.

'Here,' I say. 'But I have a flat in London.'

'Are you here working?'

'No, recovering.'

He nods. He tells me his name is Simon and he is from Harlow. He has sandy hair and blue eyes and a tender, craggy face. He walks me to my car.

'It's a shame about Milton's sister,' I say.

'Yeah. He shouldn't have left it so late,' says Simon.

The parking lot is dimly-lit and peanut shaped. Simon advances and I think he will mould me against the curve of the door. But he stops short of touching me. 'You're lovely,' he says.

I chatter. Simon nods politely, gazing steadily into my eyes and face. 'I have to go,' I say finally, and lift myself into the van, high and safe above him. He hands me a card. 'Please phone,' he says. I giggle. I take the card. I start the car and reverse quickly at a wide arc, nearly hitting a pick-up truck, stopping short. I can feel him standing still, I can feel him watching me.

O God, I do not want to die.

I phone the doctor's office from a pay phone caked with dust and the grit of the street, next to a 7–11. 'You must be patient,' the receptionist scolds. I hang up and moan into the blaring smog-shine. I will be happy for the twilight. The daylight is so large. I decide to eat.

In the 7–11, I buy cupcakes, Twinkies, Chewy Chips Ahoy, three Sprites, a beef jerky, Cheetos, Doritos, an ice-cream Chipwich and a Baby Ruth bar. I take it all home in a bulging brown bag. Mom and Larry have taken Winchell to Yosemite. I am alone with the phone and my fast food. I set it all out on one of Larry's fine Dutch plates. I take it down to my room and watch *The Oprah Winfrey Show*. The theme for today is 'How women are like their mothers.' A calm young woman sits with her hands in her lap and her hair tied back. Beside her sits an older woman with her hands in her lap and her hair tied back.

'What are some special similarities you have noticed between the two of you?' asks Oprah.

'Well,' says the daughter, 'there is one thing my mother always used to say, and now I say it too. When my husband is hardboiling an egg, I always say "you can never tell about an egg." '

'That's right,' pipes the mother, 'because of the size.'

The husband nods, looking catatonic.

I switch the channel. Donahue is doing a show on compulsive overeating. I study his wedge of white hair. It looks welded. I think, wouldn't it be funny if Crilly cut and dyed his hair the same way as Donahue, just for a laugh? A woman stands in the audience. She is obese. Donahue approaches her with his microphone. 'Phil,' she says in a faintly foreign accent, 'I really just wanted to ask a question so that my daughter could see me on television.' Donahue turns his eyes up to heaven, amused. The fat woman continues. 'I didn't *want* to stand,' she says, 'because I realise that the way I look is not the way I *should* look.' She is met by a sympathetic murmur from the audience.

I look at my plate of food, which has taken on a post-war splattered feel to it. Brown crumbs are everywhere. Cheeto crumbs blend with loose chocolate chips. Half a Twinkie lies in the middle like a capsized boat. Ice-cream from the Chipwich has seeped into everything. I squeeze my upper arm. I have gained weight since coming off methadone. I do not dare to step on the scales. I wonder how men could stand to look at me as I am now; overweight, pale, knackered. But they *do* look. At that crosstalk meeting, they were looking. But I could be wrong. Perhaps they are patronising me. Perhaps they think that I am merely a compulsive overeater posing as a heroin addict under the illusion that the latter is more glamorous. Perhaps they think I want to be Billie Holiday, and all they see really is the fat of defeat, the frazzle of sad and frenetic eyes, the haggard old sexuality buried beneath a heap of dead hope, used tin foil, Twinkies. And that Englishman was no more than a polite escort, gracing me with a glimpse of etiquette. And he probably saw my fear. And he probably hated my shirt.

I dial the doctor's office, but hang up before the receptionist answers. She would be irritated to hear my voice. And I am feeling sensitive. A hasty salesgirl or a stroppy receptionist could shatter me to bits. I hate her with all my heart.

I have keys to my father's beach house. It's warm for winter. I will drive to Malibu. This cheers me. I fill the van with green vegetables, a six pack of diet mandarin orange slice, a bathing suit, suntan oil, the AA big book, two notebooks, an assortment of pens including a Pentel set of coloured pens, a dozen cassettes, my journal, a carton of cigarettes, my address book, my green book for logging everything I have done, eaten and written on a given day, a toothbrush, a small toilet bag of expensive cosmetics, another of cheap cosmetics, and a copy of *Love in the Time of Cholera.*

I fancy the idea of travelling light. I envy the breezy French or Brazilian woman at airports who checks no luggage but flies halfway across the world with a carry-on bag. She listens to bossa nova on her headphones as the plane takes off. She listens to reggae as it lands. She has cars and men waiting for her at her destination. She lives for today. I know that excess baggage is something that I will always have. So I make certain when I leave a place and go to another that my bags, while not light, are at least complete. I think of our drive to Holyhead, complete with chemicals, including a shampoo bottle of methadone that had not been rinsed properly. It tasted of Head and Shoulders.

Now, devoid of substances, I make do with books and paper, music and clothing, heads of iceberg lettuce and NutraSweet, organisers littering the back of the van like clunky old items in the back of a thrift shop.

I drive fast down the hill, swerving too wide around steep curves, rewinding a cassette in the car stereo. When I reach the bottom, I drive west on Franklin, listening to a loud cover of 'Mas Que Nada'. Three men in a pick-up truck catch my eye and nod in approval. I smile back and speed ahead at the light, feeling bold and silly. The road is clear. By the time I reach Pacific Coast Highway, my spirits are rising. I am free. I am beautiful (in a slightly fat sort of way). I can do whatever I like. I insert a Sinead O'Connor cassette, which begins with the serenity prayer. I listen closely, rewind and listen again, this time trying to imitate her accent. I have a god. She is Irish and Catholic though I am neither. She is plump and fifty and so matronly that she could be a nurse, or a mother. She has a '50's hairdo of tight brown curls. She sports a flowered apron and a plate of fresh-baked biscuits.

Be good to yourself, she says, in a Kerry accent. Be good to yourself, and nourish yourself.

Halfway between Santa Monica and Malibu, I stop at Kentucky Fried Chicken. I order a three piece supper. The man behind the counter winks at me.

'English?' He asks.

'Well. In a way.'

'My cousin's English,' he says. 'He lives in England.'

I drive on. I drive north. At this rate, I could drive to San Francisco. I stop at a Mayfair for more sweet things. I long to feel them in the back of my mouth, in the bottom of my stomach.

My father's beach house will remain unused by anyone other than myself until the summer. I change into my mother's pink bathing suit. It is the only one I have, and it is difficult to keep myself inside it. I park myself at the edge of a dune. I sit upon the yellow blanket (belonging to my father's dog, I think) and I eat the chicken straight from the box, sandwiching the candy between my legs for later. My body is loose and flabby. I am ravenous.

The beach is empty but for a youngish couple who prance about the coastline with two small blond toddlers and three Irish setters. They are fit and sprightly. The woman has long blonde hair and blue eyes. She wears powder blue sweats and a slinky tank top. The man has sandy, shaggy hair, fashionably overgrown. His arms and chest are brown and big with muscle. The couple draws closer, calling to their dogs and children. I sit with my legs spread apart, and watch them. The man's glance falls on my makeshift feast. 'Hi,' he says doubtfully. The woman does not speak to me, but she takes note of the Kentucky fried chicken, black cupcake crumbs strewn about my towel and stretch of sand. I feel like the old drunk at the Kentish Town underground, her body draped in tea towels, pores busting from her fleshy face.

I wonder where I know the young woman from. Then I realise she is an actress, a famous one. 'Fluffy!' she shouts to one of the dogs. And the man, I have seen him also. I squint to be sure. I consider what to do. Should I take the chicken into the house and pretend I have not been eating it? Should I introduce myself anyway, as we are clearly neighbours? Should I mention my father's latest soap? The couple retreat into their house, and return with two paddles and a ball. But they've seen me now. If I talk to them, they might see I am intelligent and forget about the fat and food. Then again, they might scorn or pity me. I know they are concerned about the environment. I've seen both of them appear on a *Stars Supporting the Earth* special on ABC. Should I express some concern for the earth and apologise for purchasing food from a place that wastes paper? They play paddleball on the beach. The small blond boys run about with their dogs, nearing the water and pulling away. After a while, I eat again. I do not throw the box away. I do not attempt to conceal it. I eat straight from it, and when I am finished, I finish the cupcake, while the twosome play paddleball not ten feet away, skipping and jumping to meet the ball and pausing only to call out the score.

rain

It is the kind of day I love to be inside of. Los Angeles is concave and crisp; a basin of cloud and blue-lipped sea, and the road is slick from fresh winter rain. I like the *whoosh*; quick wet sounds in my van of the metallic skin. I stretch my neck to catch the city winking between the high palm trees. A steel-blue line contains the new sky, a ceiling that gapes and shines like enamel. There is no thunder, just a silent crack and the rain falls to the earth in downy slivers. A wet sheet of March. It smells of paste and Plasticine, like nursery school in New York, like the clandestine hushes of children during naptime, united in the wake of a black and blue sky. (We played not against the rain, but because of it.) I have always loved the rain.

In L.A., rain is a gift. It clears the smog and makes it glisten with a hangover wet which clings to the sleeves of the city. No one wears shorts or Ray-Bans (at least no one I can see) and the shopkeepers discuss the weather, no less than they would do in Yorkshire or Lancashire.

I want to have some alterations done; hems and things. I gather my things and walk around the house with my arms full, not knowing what to do first. I throw them on the bed. I make for the telephone. I do not hesitate before I dial. I have had enough of prayer.

Claudia here. I need to know, now.

And in a sensible and condescending tone comes Yes,

Claudia, you're in the clear. You have no venereal diseases, no cervical or ovarian cancer.

But what about the HIV? The HIV.

You are negative and in the clear.

I hang up the phone and weep a little. I wish I was Catholic so that I could say something lyrical and gracious. I do my best. The Lord's Prayer, though I can only remember some of the words. I will have my alterations done once and for all.

It is not cold. My car is fierce and clean. It winks at me with droplets. I unlock it and enter it and steer its rear end round and pelt up the hill to the market.

At the dry-cleaning place, I try on two pairs of black trousers, a summer dress and a black shirt for the Japanese lady to shorten. It takes a while. She is grave as she takes my measurements, confirming each inch aloud. She is an attractive woman of about fifty, with a full mane of black hair in a chunky bun. She wears a floral-print blouse. I give her garments for dry-cleaning. She says she will have to be careful with my dinner dress, due to a fragile row of deco-type buttons. I don't really care what happens to it. She makes a note in red marker and attaches it to the dinner dress. 'Careful of buttons' the note says. The rain turns sleety and rectangular against the window. The lady runs outside. 'It snow!' she shouts. 'It snow!' A square-jawed actor passes by on a wet run. 'First time!' She cries to him. He smiles at her, nods. 'First time it snow!' She looks at me and repeats this. 'First time in sixteen year!' Yes, I nod, it is true. She is very happy. She is ecstatic.

In the beachwood market I buy things for Elana, who lies at home in bed with flu. Cookies and carbonated drinks to soothe the stomach. A sketch pad and a large box of crayons. Edna is the checkout lady. She is sixty or so, with glasses and bleached curly hair which is full today with puff and humidity. She wears pastel slacks and fake Reese's peanut butter cup earrings that her grandchildren gave her.

Edna has a dry expression like the ladies on *Coronation Street*, and is not the sort of elderly lady whom one can't swear in front of. Her voice is husky.

'It's snowing,' I tell her.

'I know,' she says, pleased.

'The woman next door was very excited,' I say. Edna looks up.

'She's a nice lady,' she says. 'A very nice lady.'

'Yes. There used to be a guy who worked there. I didn't like him.'

'Oh!' Edna cries. 'What a schmuck he was!'

Homer, the bag boy, puts my things into a bag. 'I hated that guy,' he says. 'I remember him bitching at people all the time, and playing baseball with himself in the street!'

'That's right.'

As I drive up the hill and back down again, palm trees blow in a vinyl way, and the sky is growing deep and lavender, fermenting with the coming night. I have taken my things to be altered at last, and it took no time at all.

i see you on the prince of wales road

I have been clean for five months now. I live in a bungalow on the beach. Crilly phones from a rehab in Leicester.

'I'm realising a fuck of a lot of things,' he tells me. I imagine him standing in the rec room with a handful of ten pence coins. And his eyes startled and clear, his pupils large. I ask him what he has learned.

'About how I've hurt you. How I've hurt me own self. You know, since I met you, I've made all of myself into you. My identity was based on being your boyfriend. When you stopped being unfaithful to me, I really put meself into it. It was just you.'

'And heroin.'

'And heroin. You know, I've thought about Cat O'Fun. Why he died. I figure it was loneliness that killed him. And despondence. We were so scared and sad; we filled him with despondence. And then we went away, and he died.'

'Since when did you start using words like "despondence"?'

'Don't take the piss, Claudia. I'm trying to talk to you.'

'All right, I'm sorry. Yes, I've thought the same thing.'

'And we was dyin', Claudia. Me n' you.'

'We were.'

'I think about you all the time.'

'Are there women there?'

'No.'

'All those men going out of their mind. Do you sit round and talk about women? Do you tell crude stories?'

'You know I don't talk that way.'

'And the others? Don't they say lewd things, like in prison?'

'Not in front of me, they don't. I'm house leader, you know. At any slight display of misogyny, I level with them. I say, "I don't like that kind of talk".'

He would too. I laugh. I look to the ocean. A swarm of dolphins frolic on the tide, silhouetted in the high waves, flapping their fins. I tell Crilly about the dolphins.

'What's the head of the place like?' I ask. 'Do you like him?'

'It's a woman. She's old. She's tough, caustic. Extremely fuckin' wise.'

'She must think you're really sweet.'

'No,' he says, his voice rising, 'she thinks I'm really positive.'

In the afternoon I phone Anita who is looking after my flat in London. She assures me that the flat is fine; several stray junkies have been lurking round the front so she has had security grilles put on the windows. The neons are intact. The upstairs neighbours are moving to Australia.

'Oh, and by the way,' she says, 'you know that woman you and Crilly used to hang out with sometimes? The Irish one, who worked at the pub?'

'Maggie.'

'That's right. Well, I saw her on the bus just last week; she asked after you and Crilly. I pretended I didn't know anything.'

'Good.'

'She looked terrible; emaciated and spotty, her hair all stringy. She asked me to join her for a drink, but I didn't.'

'Good.'

'Anyway, they found her in the subway underpass at Swiss Cottage.'

'What do you mean?'

'I saw a photo of her in the *New Camden Journal*. The caption said that she was completely blue by the time they found her.'

'What?'

'She died of an overdose, it said. She had nothing on her but a syringe; it took them a while even to identify her.'

'Are you sure it was her?'

'Maggie Delaney, it said, of Malahide, Ireland. They shipped her body back to Dublin.'

I fall silent.

'Claudia? Are you all right?'

'Of course.'

'I didn't think you would be surprised.'

'I don't know if I'm surprised or not.'

'You never liked her.'

'I tried to like her.'

'She upset you.'

'She did.' I am stunned. 'Are you sure it was her?'

'Yes.'

'Why would she OD?'

'How should I know.'

'You just saw her, didn't you?'

'Yes, but . . .'

'I suppose Crilly doesn't know yet.'

'It just happened.'

'And here I was, thinking she would be around forever, like a skunk. She never used needles. She was just like us.'

'No,' says Anita, 'she wasn't.'

'You know, she was a stupid bitch sometimes. When Crilly was in prison, she made my life miserable.'

'I know.'

I feel stupid, but I continue to talk, though I know it's babble. 'She was a right devious cunt, Anita. She would have given the world just to keep Crilly in junk.'

'I know.'

'She was a real waster, that one. A dead loss.'

Tonight I write to Crilly. I lie awake in my bed, listening to the waves. I write a poem about dolphins. I read from my *Belfast: War as a Way of Life* book. I do not think of Maggie.

The following morning, I awake early and swing in the hammock. I remember small particulars that Crilly told me; Maggie had three sisters. She once wrote an article for her school paper, about bees. She lived with her mother but preferred her aunt.

I search the summer sea for dolphins. I forget all about her.

But . . . you are in my thoughts when I sleep, Maggie. Your body withered and blue. Your blue jeans fastened and your shirt-tails tucked in tight as they always were. Only your sleeve is ruffled, shoved past the elbow. How I hate you! You weakling. You whore. You silly smackhead. Your lips fat with affectation. Your head muddled and heavy with skag. Your silly pinpoint eyes. Your vacuous, swimming, pathetic pools of blue. Blue as your dead skin. Blue, blue, as blue as the face on you. Your rag-and-bone nails and skinny hands of screaming white. Don't ring, Maggie. Don't talk to my machine. I see you on the Prince of Wales Road. You are walking my way with a dealer named Sport. You are sheathed in black and your freckles are pale and many. You are still now, but a fence of tatty barbed wire courts and crevices behind you . . . You are still now, but a fence of tatty barbed wire courts and crevices behind you . . . you are still now, but a fence of tatty barbed wire . . . courting . . . crevicing . . .

Still now.

Still.

On my way to a meeting, I walk through the park alone. When it was still light, old Polish immigrants sat on benches with grandchildren and snacks in paper bags, but I have missed them. A one-legged man hobbles past. A frayed lady in a shower cap walks an emaciated Dalmatian on a lead. She stops and asks me, 'Have you seen my other dog?' I shake my head. Broken trees cast shadows on the path. As I draw closer to the rec centre, big band music booms from an auditorium. Through a lit doorway, I see them playing in a wide semi-circle; young people in starched white shirts with tubas and horns. Parallel to the auditorium, in another room fronted by boxy windows, elderly people dance. At first it seems they are dancing to the big band in the next room. Yet as I peer through the biggest window, I see that they move in circles and swing one another by the arms, as though square-dancing. A man stands by a phonograph, speaking into a microphone. He is fat with a full head of wedged blond hair and a moustache. He is an overstuffed, toupeed Marlboro man in a cowboy shirt. Faintly, beneath the loud '40s music booming through the walls, I make out the banjo sound of a country jig. A record rotates on the phonograph. Some of the dancers are handicapped, and they move slow and steadily, switching partners in time to the music, doing the two-step in a cluster and moving out to allow couples through an even row. A skinny, bespectacled black man in a plaid suit dances with a short, pear-bodied white woman with thinning hair, wearing a ruffled magenta skirt. An elderly Korean man, wearing a cowboy shirt of turquoise, swings a Mexican woman with tree-stump thighs and a grey bouffant. She wears a tiered, ruffled dress that fans stiffly about her like straw. An ancient lady sporting Western saloon 'vamp' wear makes her way alone across the room, taking painstaking steps with the aid of a walker. As skirts fan out, puffed by crinoline, they expose control-top pantyhose and the tops of girdled legs. Cloth roses rise and fall above heaving bosoms. White, dyed, and fine hair is teased into severe curves held above the head, or low gelled hooks above the shoulder, curls that do not move. I wonder how they can dance in time to the record when the big band music is so loud. They seem to know the steps very well. The record is heavy on ukelele. The leader sings along:

> . . . . Walk down to the corner store,
> watch my baby, she's a comin'
> Lord my heart is broke in two
> Hallelujah to the poor
> man who sings a song so blue.
> Say hey darlin' can't you see
> Judgement time is surely comin'
> sorry sight, a man like me
> who loves a woman he can't see . . . Amen!

And the old people dance, though the horns from next door relent, a cacophony of brass. I stand watching for awhile, watching through the big window. A park local approaches and stands beside me.

'They can't do it,' he says presently. 'Ain't no one who can.' I nod as though I understand him. I guess it's time to leave, but I'm not so sure I want to.

Though he is short, Jimmy K. has a long, sinewy body, all lank and lean, and he wears his long black hair in a pony tail. He has a narrow face of shadowy olive features, and his lashes are long. He wears a T-shirt that reads 'The Future is Stupid' and his jeans are pale and tattered and missing at the knee. He is effeminate, though he doesn't like people to think so, and he is often draped over the shoulders and backs of women like one of those clingy stuffed-bear knapsacks bought on holiday in Miami. He speaks in a Latin accent of some kind, though it is so exaggerated that it does not betray his actual race. My suspicion is that he was born and raised in Los Angeles of South American parents, and in his sobriety, he has conducted a search for his routes, rendering him a sort of Hispanic caricature. Instead of saying, 'I'm Jimmy and I'm an addict,' he stands proudly before the group and says 'I'm Jeemy and I don't dreenk or use no matter what.' His declaration is so familiar to the West Hollywood meetings that when he makes it, we all say it with him.

'Hello, I'm Jeemy, I don't dreenk or use no matter what,' he declares this evening at the rec centre, swaggering as if he were drunk, though of course he isn't.

'Hello, Jimmy,' we say, in unison.

'I'm having some troble weeth my room-mates at the moment. The problem ees that I hate them. I pray for thees defect to be removed, but I'm not sure I wanna it to be removed. I hate them. Sometimes, I write what I'm feelin' on a sleep of paper, and leave eet around the apartment and forget. Some-times my room-mates, these two girls of whom I hate, see the paper and they write what they feel on top of what I feel. Like yesterday, I write on a sleep of paper, "I feel like shit", and thees mornin', I awake up and I see the paper, and it says "You are shit!" And when I do something deesgusting amongst them, they say, "Leave the room!" I hate them. I really hate them. That's all I wish to share.'

Jimmy steps off the podium. We applaud. A professional woman takes the stand. In her hand she holds a basket of plastic chips, like the things they gamble with in Las Vegas.

'We give chips at this meeting for lengths of sobriety,' she says. 'Would anyone like to take a newcomer's chip?'

A plump black man takes a purple chip. He is perspiring heavily and holds a handkerchief in his hand.

'My biggest problem is acquiring a higher power,' he tells us. 'I was raised as a Baptist and then I became an atheist. My sponsor gave me an exercise, told me to write about the person in my life who I thought was more spiritual than anybody, and then to pray to the image of that person. I thought hard and I chose Charlie Parker. Then my sponsor told me I had co-dependent issues, what with Charlie Parker being a heroin addict and all. So I chose my mother. Thanks Mom!'

The newcomer waves the chip at us and descends from the podium to wild applause. The chip woman asks if there is anybody with thirty days. Nobody. Sixty days. One middle-aged woman in a brown suit takes a chip, says thanks, and sits down again. There is nobody for ninety days.

'Six months?'

I cough and make my way to the podium. As I walk, people applaud. I have promised myself I will make a speech at six months, and I have rehearsed it. How I feel. What I intend to do with my life. Who I am grateful to, like the Oscars. Instead I stand before the crowd, clear my throat and take a deep breath. I don't know what the fuck I'm going to say.

'About a year and a half ago . . .' I begin, looking at the faces. I see people I know. I see people I do not know. 'A year and a half ago I was so afraid of daylight that I could not get out of bed before dark. The sight of light made me cringe so I stayed in bed, watching the worst telly I could watch . . . Australian soaps . . . eating those white chocolate mouses from Woolworth's . . . I mean you don't have those here I know — you have Woolworth's but not the white chocolate mouses . . .'

Someone laughs. I glance in their direction.

'I didn't know my body at all,' I continue, 'my body was not mine to know. I became five months pregnant without realising it. I had to have a special abortion. When I awoke from the operation, I asked the nurse, "Was it a girl or a boy?" She told me to get some sleep. The thing is . . . well, the thing is, I forgot all about that part. I forgot. Until now.'

No one stirs. I clear my throat.

'When my boyfriend brought me home, we drew the curtains and went right to bed. He brought us heroin. We didn't answer the phone or the door. I don't remember how long this went on. I think it went on for a year.'

My face is hot. I touch my cheeks, feeling for the tears or sweat, but they are dry. Just hot.

'But we never spoke of it afterwards. We never mentioned the baby. It just didn't seem important . . . And now . . . now I can feel the sex of my child. I can feel her inside of me, I can feel her in my arms. I want to say goodbye to her. I want to wish her well.'

The room is too still. It frightens me.

'I want to wish my baby well.' The chip woman puts the basket down but for one blue chip reading 'Six Months'. She hands it to me. She holds me. I let out a long breath and clutch the plastic tight, very tight, inside my hand.

i promise i'll be good

On this beach in the sea so swirly and salty and amorous with kelp and dolphins, I stand to my neck and the water fills every gap, between my thighs, between my breasts, the puffed tented coves of my swimsuit, the line between my legs and open pores everywhere, immersed, wet. I am alone in the sea today, sheltered by the rocky cliffs to my left and right. Dick the surfer has not surfaced nor lounged in his terrace hammock, to leer at the surf or remark on my suntan, saying, Hey Claude if you get any darker there I'll have to stop wearing shades.

Hey, I'm brown all over. For breakfast I had oatmeal with milk and NutraSweet; it was fantastic. It is almost time for lunch. I smoke menthol cigarettes. They fill my lungs with eucalyptus; at least they *feel* healthy. I smoke on the beach. When I emerge from the water, I make notes on my essay. I write long essays for no one in particular. I write about London. And the sun licks my skin dry and kisses me everywhere, my gigantic buddy of a sun, so cheeky, so immense, a show-off of a sunflower punching through the sky.

Today is the day of the Notting Hill carnival. I spoke to Anita earlier; she will be going. She'll buy one of those whistles with the Jamaican colours on the band; she'll wear it round her neck and shimmy through the crowd, her eyes lazy on cherubic children perched high on daddies' shoulders, and the carousel floats shouting salsa and calypso, sporting such obscenity of colour, those pinks, those yellows, those laughing limes.

Londoners dressed like Latiners in scarlet crinoline skirts, no stockings, shoulders bare, necks and chests dressed with sweat, the summerest sweat. Whites forging dreadlocks from the finest hair upon their heads, *trying* to be black, *wishing* they were black, if only this once. I remember Notting Hill. I went there. Once. Twice. Several times. To the carnival. I erupted from the tube with my eager body plastered to the others, the other eagers, the goers, all going and running to the carnival.

In the ocean, now, I think of this. I am not sad. Breakfast was good. The beach is better. Catalina lurks before me somewhere, caked in bits of mist. The water is a reward; it heals and seduces like something knowing, the way it oozes about, in and out of everywhere. It is omniscient. I enjoy the tininess, the insignificance of me all alone in God's great ocean bath, drenched with the wet of it and so diminutive. But I can think of London, if I want to. I can dream.

I think of pubs, or maybe one pub, that one in Newington Green where I used to watch the Ska bands, bouncing up and down like a fleshy fool of a yo-yo in my wooden seat. And all that smoke, twirling in the yellow light. The dance floor is bare but for six tall lesbians, at least three of them Australian, tearing across the floor, holding their elbows high like soldiers, charging at each other with amazing speed, their bodies taking so much space, and more space still when they leap to the shameless clash and horns, knees high in the air, palms stretched out like hallelujah palms, or fists clenched, mock-boxing: go at her body and stop before you hit, recoil your fists every second beat. I don't dare to join them with my silly curly hair and my eye make-up, but I watch them, I bounce. Someone smiles at me. He likes the trite simple girlyness of me. I smile back. Not because I am interested; I smile to be smiled at. The horns cavort, all those horns, players pointed and fuzzy and three in a row like tea cosies that match.

If I keep my body clean and my eyes open, can't I come back? If I promise to wake before ten and get a job, memorise the names of vendors at the local fruit stand and newsagent and pet shop and laundromat, can't I come back? I promise I will be good. Lovely though the sea and sand is, cleansing as milk though the sun is, streaky and bleak though the anthracite English streets in winter are and will be, I want to come back, I want to go home.

Please.

I want to go home.

When I emerge from the doctor's office, I am dragging like a muggy morning and I can barely make it across the street. I stick gum in my mouth while jaywalking, and I chew until it is hard and ropey. My car is parked in a leafy backstreet.

In the car, I slide the front seat down flat with myself upon it, my head on the headrest and my eyes closed. If I open my eyes slightly, I can see the trees swaying a bit against an overcast sky and I have cause to think of England. And there are birds. My earrings weigh heavily until I take them off. I am so very tired.

When I begin to drive, I can think of nowhere to go. I have a meeting, but not for ninety minutes. I have a ticket to Britain, but not for a week. There is no food nor drink to be consumed in the interim; there's too much weight, the post-methadone weight. So I simply head west. I feel below my eyes for circles and though I cannot see them in the rear-view mirror I can feel them in my face like gashes struck by daylight fatigue, or violent blows delivered into unsuspecting slumber. Traffic streams on all sides of me in monotonous rows but I cannot hear the sound of it, above a kind of road drone which lies beneath my car and through my head. Police cars do not stir me. I plod dully through intersections, pausing only to stop or turn. I am looking for a coffee shop within which to park myself but feeling my body, newly abstinent from starch or snacks, and lumplike besides, I have little desire to stop. I drive. And the traffic grows slower, and thicker. In the slug of a fume-choked day, I allow myself a slim fantasy.

... I am driving just past the brink of dawn onto the North Circular Road in London, England. My car is immersed in rare March fog; my windows are damp and lightly steamed and I am fresh like steamed squash. My lover is in exile and I have left my friend at home. I do not stop at the petrol station for Marathon bars or cheesy stuff. I have no travelling things. My neck smells lightly of citrus cologne and my hair is newly washed. I wear no jewellery. I am slender and snug in my driver's seat. The fog is clearing towards Hertfordshire. I take the M1 without words in my head. My skin is moist and I sense an inward trickle — a sweet dewy grief in my heart, mild and compact as poppy seeds. The M1 is empty but for a lorry or two sporting burly Midlands men grinning and showing Yorkie bars from their teeth. I do not wave but I smile. I am not tired. I touch my face and I can feel that it is lovely like a flat and flawless stone. I can drive at my best speed without fear of police or pursuit. I can drive until the speeding signs are no longer there by the roadside. I will not stop. I can drive to where the steel mills are archaic and forbidding, large and unused. I can drive to outer Bradford where the smell of chicken korma is strong and Pakistanis linger on cobbled streets before old houses the colour of rust and magenta and burnt orange. I can drive to the borders — Berwick-upon-Tweed, where English green dissolves to Scottish gold, and exuberant hills dance coquettishly by my side, aligned by nothing but a slice of sea which shimmers at the kiss of nightfall. I can drive through Glencoe where clan battles have raged and mountains tempt me to steep and ominous heights, spectacular and strange and, impressed though I am, I will drive beyond. I will drive to the Highland lochs and rocks stark and striking like a cavernous nirvana on the moon, and further still I will drive beyond. I can drive to the northernmost tip of this long little island, to the blessed bonny tip, where nothing lies before me but the sea and a ferry bound for the Shetlands. I will stand on the tip, facing the sea and Scandinavia, thinking of Vikings and the people I love.

I have driven to the tip and I will stand here; I am standing here, standing here and looking out. And once I have stood here I will drive beyond, again, further beyond, again, now, beyond. Into that vast and unchangeable sky. And even there, I will not stop.

In memory of Vincent

Founded in 1986, Serpent's Tail publishes the innovative and the challenging.

If you would like to receive a catalogue of our current publications please write to:

FREEPOST
Serpent's Tail
4 Blackstock Mews
LONDON N4 2BR

(No stamp necessary if your letter is posted in the United Kingdom.)

Absence Makes the Heart
Lynne Tillman

'In *Absence Makes the Heart* Lynne Tillman lures us onto unfamiliar ground with utterly persuasive, utterly duplicitous candor. Once there, we shall never be brought safely home. Her writing leaves our assumptions about life and art a shambles and, because it is funny and revealing, we relish it; but, reader, beware — you will be getting more than you either expect or deserve.'   HARRY MATHEWS

'Lynne Tillman has the strongest, smartest, most subtly distinct writer's voice of my generation. I admire her breadth of observation, her syntax, her wit.'   GARY INDIANA

'These bizarre short stories make alluring reading.'
                                                    Time Out

Ocean Avenue
Margaret Wilkinson

"In her first novel, Wilkinson confidently and evocatively blends the historical and personal . . . into a disturbing yet funny tale."　　*Publishers Weekly*

"Wilkinson's original, witty, insightful novel has a surreal quality. Her characters are sad, hilarious, wonderful."　　*Jewish Chronicle*

"An impressive debut."　　*She*

"Through it all there glows a sense of place, of history and identity combined with a wistful wryness."　　*Sunday Times*

"*Ocean Avenue* is like a photograph album, each chapter a cameo portrait of a member of the family, an event in the family history, each staking its claim to attention. 'It was talking with authority about the human heart that intrigued me. Like novels,' says the narrator. *Ocean Avenue* is both authoritative and tentative in its approach to the heart: serious in intent, self-deprecatingly, affectionately funny in the telling."　　GILLIAN ALLNUTT

Transmission
Atima Srivastava

"The plot of *Transmission* is perfectly formed, and the characters strong . . . a fast, complicated book."
The Independent

"A compulsive look at straight, young non-drug users with HIV, inter-racial relationships and the ethics of working in TV . . . A socially-conscious London novel that refuses to take itself too seriously."
The Face

"Comedy that is both bleak and tender, sharp-edged portraits of media makers and monsters, a wry look at urban styles of love and survival by a born story-teller."
MICHÈLE ROBERTS

"*Transmission* is a new novel that has everything: sex, glamour, politics, friendship, excitement, and a conscience."
Northern Star

"The writing is sharp and punchy . . . while the engaging descriptions of Angie's cross-cultural family life provide a wealth of insights into British ethnic experience. The novel's major strength, though, is in steering clear of either sermonising or trivialising while exploring difficult and challenging subjects."
Scotland on Sunday

"This is the first great novel of 1992!"
Events South West

Alex Wants to Call It Love
Silvia Sanza

"The characters alternately search for connection and long for solitude; Sanza is adept at conveying the frustrations of failed intimacy and the rarity of true communication between even the closest of friends."
Publishers Weekly

"Sanza's debut is cute and observant in targeting the vacuity of urban life."   *The Independent on Sunday*

"Crushes unwanted characters like cockroaches, but it still manages to reclaim Lower Manhattan for the human race. It bounces on a rich diet of gall and schmaltz, cheerfully cushioned by 'the humour of getting by.' The low-life scrapes mask high-minded aims. Large ideas – about chaos and the art that tames it – sneak up through the wisecracks."
The Observer

"*Slaves of New York*, Sanza style."   *Elle*

"Explores death, love, work, writing and why people do all these things. Silvia Sanza writes from an original and exciting angle that keeps you surprised and, ultimately, satisfied."   KATE PULLINGER

"Alex may want to call it love but Silvia Sanza is more likely to diagnose lustful anomie. With her bleak precision and Martini-dry wit, she tells things exactly as they are and does so mercilessly. Required reading for the intelligent disaffected."
PATRICK GALE

Nudists May Be Encountered
Mary Scott

"Tales of distinctive wit and sharp social comment . . .
a neat catalogue of folly and pretence."

The Sunday Times

"Elegant, observant and smart, with serious mania,
misery and experimentalism lurking just underneath." *City Limits*

"The characters in these wry, intelligent stories are
frantically trying to fend off despair."

Publishers Weekly

"[A] fresh, witty and ironic first collection of stories
. . . some have a dreamy, surreal edge; others are
brash and sardonic . . . Scott is a real literary artist
and totally accessible. I'm looking forward to reading
more by her." *East Bay Express*

"Mary Scott's stories are sharp, clear, funny and
smart. They're also finely constructed and as I read
them (with great enjoyment) I felt in the presence of a
confident new writer with a truly fresh way of
writing." MALCOLM BRADBURY

"By understanding the enormity of life's minutiae
and by describing with unerring accuracy the
struggle between individuals and a virtually cosmic
notion of bureaucracy, Mary Scott delivers a
collection of stories which are as funny as they are
unsettling and as well observed as they are ingenious.
With such a grasp of irony and understatement there
seems little doubt that *Nudists May Be Encountered*
will establish Mary Scott as a vital and original new
writer." MICHAEL BRACEWELL